Scottish
Bakehouse
Mysteries™

Reign of Terrier

Jan Fields

Annie's®
AnniesFiction.com

Books in the Scottish Bakehouse Mysteries series

The Jig Is Up
If Looks Could Kilt
A Reel Threat
Lass and Found
Silence of the Clans
Shepherd's Lie
A Faerie Dangerous Game
Tartan Feathered
Yule Be Sorry
Of Ice and Men
Reign of Terrier
Aye for an Aye
From Plaid to Worse
Quill the Messenger
Under Loch and Key
Paying the Piper
Isle and Tribulation
Scone Cold Murder
A Hopeless Ness
Settling Auld Scores
A Lass Resort
Heid and Seek

. . . and more to come!

Library of Congress-in-Publication Data
Reign of Terrier / by Jan Fields
p. cm.
I. Title
                    2020941676

AnniesFiction.com
(800) 282-6643
Scottish Bakehouse Mysteries™
Series Creator: Shari Lohner
Series Editor: Elizabeth Morrissey
Cover Illustrator: Kelley McMorris

10 11 12 13 14 | Printed in China | 9 8 7 6 5 4 3 2

1

As Molly Ferris scanned the empty front room of Bread on Arrival, she marveled afresh at how the bakehouse was transformed daily from the lively bustle of morning to the quiet of closing time. Some days the last customers faced closing time reluctantly, nursing a coffee and perhaps a scone, cranachan, or Abernethy biscuit at one of the rustic café tables beside the softly crackling fire in the stone fireplace. Today, the room had actually emptied well before it was time to lock the front door.

As always, the sight of the cozy grouping of tables with their engraved Celtic knots made Molly happy with the choice she had made with her best friends and business partners, Laura Donovan and Carol MacCallan, to open a bakery together. The chairs reminded Molly of the people of Loch Mallaig, Michigan—a little rough, but wearing their background and heritage proudly. The beautiful wood-and-glass displays went well with the tables. They weren't rustic, but they had an aura of well-maintained age that felt right for the old Victorian-turned-bakehouse.

Across the room, Bridget Ross flipped the sign on the door from *Open* to *Closed*, then approached Molly, her face concerned. "I could stay a little longer and help clean up," she offered. "I hate to bail early." The young woman's shoulder-length black hair was pulled into a high ponytail that barely showed off the streak of lavender running through it. Molly thought of it as Bridget's one wild streak.

Though an only child, Bridget Ross was far from the spoiled, self-indulgent stereotype Molly sometimes heard people grumble about. Of course, Molly's own twentysomething daughter, Chloe, was an only child, and Molly couldn't think of anyone who worked harder. Bridget had been an asset to Bread on Arrival from the day they hired her. She took her part-time job seriously, and the customers adored the pleasant young woman.

Molly came around the counter with Bridget's backpack and heavy raincoat. "Go," she said. "You'll be late for your class if you keep lollygagging around here, especially in this weather." All day, the weather had shifted between snow and icy rain, making any time outside miserable. "I can sweep and wipe tables with no problem. And you said this professor doesn't appreciate latecomers."

Bridget rolled her eyes. "He definitely doesn't. One time, he actually threw chalk at a guy for coming in halfway through a lecture. Who even uses chalk anymore?"

"Then you'd better go," Molly said. "You don't need to duck chalk on our behalf. Have a good class."

Bridget grinned, her normal cheerfulness restored. "If you're sure. I do love these Monday afternoon forensic science lectures. They're fascinating."

Molly opened the door. "Best be on your way then."

Bridget went, while Molly watched her fondly. Working around Bridget's college schedule was never a problem, but sometimes it was clear Bridget worried she was being too demanding. Molly shook her head. *That girl couldn't be demanding if she tried.*

Molly hummed softly under her breath as she walked to the doorway that led from the front of the bakehouse into the back hallway. She'd tucked a broom right behind the doorframe so it would be handy while out of the customer's line of sight.

Laura often said that cleaning was something customers imagined being done by elves in the night, so it was best to keep it out of their sight. That was something Laura had picked up as head chef of a trendy restaurant in New York. Molly wasn't sure the Loch Mallaig residents were quite as picky as that, but she was happy enough to follow Laura's greater experience.

She had finished sweeping and was carefully wiping down the last of the tables when she heard the scamper of claws on the wood floor. Molly glanced up to see her Scottish terrier, Angus, dashing toward her with Carol right behind him.

"I took out the kitchen trash, and Angus rushed down the outside stairs from the apartment and gave me *the look* from the other side of the fenced yard," Carol said. "You know full well that I'm a sucker for the look. I can't even resist it when my chickens do it."

Molly laughed. She couldn't imagine chickens managing the winsome expression that her Scottie excelled at. "You're a soft touch."

"Maybe." Carol grinned at her. "I'm done cleaning the kitchen, so I'm heading out. Laura should be proud of us. We managed to survive today and Saturday with her gone, even with Valentine's Day looming."

"I'm still not sure Laura wants to hear about how much we didn't need her," Molly said. Laura had taken a rare break to spend the weekend with her family in Marquette. In addition to visiting her parents, now in their seventies, and her brother, Brody, and his family, she was also going to do some shopping and check out a new organic fruit wholesaler. Bread on Arrival bought as much locally grown produce as possible, but February in the Upper Peninsula was not a time for local bounty. "We should probably tell her that we struggled a bit."

"Maybe." Carol pulled her phone from her pocket. "I'd better let Harvey know I'm going to be late since I've got to stop and pick up something for supper. Maisie and Gavin were over a lot this weekend, and the cupboard has a bad case of Old Mother Hubbard. I'm constantly amazed by how much children can eat."

Molly felt the smallest pang at not having anyone who would miss her if she were coming home late, nor a rush of grandkids to eat her out of house and home. But then Angus plopped his warm little body down on one of her feet and gazed up at her expectantly. She knew he was waiting for his dinner and she mentally amended her thoughts. *I always have you, don't I?*

"Ooh, Beverly Scott sent me a text about that new bookstore outside town," Carol said. "What's its name again?"

"The one selling used books?" Molly asked. She struggled to conjure the name for a moment, then it finally popped into her brain. "Books & Bargains."

"Ah yes, that's it. Beverly popped in there on her lunch break and found a book of unusual knitting patterns." Carol held up the phone to show off a photo of a slightly worn book with a beautiful blanket on the cover. "We were talking about this very thing at the last Fair Knitting Ladies meeting."

"It was nice of her to think of you."

Carol nodded and continued reading the text. "She says she put it on hold for me with the owner. She would have bought it for me, but she didn't want to presume I'd want it. I definitely do." She glanced at the time. "And I bet they're still open."

"I've been meaning to check out that bookshop," Molly said. "But it's rather off my beaten path."

"Why don't you come along? If the weather doesn't bother you, that is. I can't believe it's actually raining this time of year instead of snowing. I imagine the blizzard is waiting in the wings."

"Bite your tongue," Molly scolded mildly, but Carol had a point. Living in Michigan's Upper Peninsula meant February was wall-to-wall snow, so the rain had been an unseasonable surprise that no one expected to last.

Carol went on as if she hadn't heard Molly's scolding. "Actually, I'd appreciate having your extra set of eyes in this mess. The roads can be dark early at that end of town with all the trees. I'd ask Harvey, but the conditions are only going to get worse if I waste time driving home first."

"I'm game." Molly glanced down at Angus. "Sorry, dinner will have to wait."

As if he understood, the little dog drooped visibly before aiming his shiny black eyes toward her again.

"Nope," Molly said. "I am immune to the puppy eyes. I promise you won't starve, and I'll give you a little treat before we go."

At the word "treat," Angus perked back up.

"Let me get Angus settled and grab my coat," Molly said. "Then I'll be ready to go."

The new bookshop was in a residential neighborhood outside Loch Mallaig's business district. It was far from the cheery storefronts whose displays mixed the Scottish plaids and bagpipes that heralded the Scottish town's heritage with the moose, bear, and wolf motifs popular throughout the Upper Peninsula.

"Why would anyone put a business out here?" Molly asked as she watched for the address, finding it difficult to see in the rain and early darkness.

"I imagine it'll do fine," Carol replied. As Molly had done, she leaned forward as if closeness to the windshield would help cut through the gloom. "The owner was smart putting the word 'Bargains' in the name of the shop. It'll draw folks like bees to honey. Assuming there actually are bargains. Which we are about to find out." Carol pointed ahead.

They had reached the old farmhouse that now held a bookstore. Molly peered through the windshield at the cold drizzle and hugged her raincoat around her before hopping out and racing with Carol from the parking lot to the farmhouse's wide front porch.

Once under the shelter of the porch roof, Molly and Carol shook off as much rain as they could. Carol leaned her umbrella against a wicker chair to avoid taking it inside and dripping on the floor. As they went in, a jangle of bells announced them, and a stork-like man with a shock of snow-white hair came around a corner. "May I help you ladies?"

"I'm Carol MacCallan and this is Molly Ferris," Carol said. "We're from Bread on Arrival."

"Ah yes, I've heard your bakehouse has the best scones this side of Scotland," the man said. "I'm afraid I haven't had time to drop in yet. I've been quite busy getting my shop set up."

Molly glanced around the foyer, which had several doorways leading off of it. The cozy farmhouse was a warren of small rooms, perfect for a used bookshop, and she spotted comfy chairs here and there. "It's quite an undertaking, but you've done a wonderful job so far."

The man's smile brightened his otherwise somber face. He held out his hand. "I'm Edgar Richardson. Call me Ed. And welcome to Books & Bargains." They all shook hands, then he peered at Carol. "Carol MacCallan, you said? Beverly Scott asked me to hold a book for you earlier. I have it up at the register."

"Thank you," Carol said. "Though I wouldn't mind poking around a bit before I check out."

"Certainly. You may find more knitting books in the craft section." Ed gestured to a doorway. "Through there and to the right."

"Go ahead, Carol," Molly encouraged. "I'll be happy to browse."

"I'll try not to get lost," Carol said with a grin before following Ed's directions into the next room.

Molly scanned the entryway, which boasted two narrow bookshelves, both reaching up to the high ceiling. "How does one shop up there?" She pointed toward a high shelf full of books.

"Those are the books that are waiting for a little TLC," Ed said. "I took some book restoration classes in Detroit as I dreamed of this place. So far, I haven't had time to get to them, but I will."

"That's probably a valuable skill for a used bookseller." Molly glanced around again. "Is the shop just the downstairs, or do you have retail space upstairs too?"

Ed chuckled. "The second floor isn't fit for public viewing, I'm afraid. I recommend staying down here unless you want to see the collection of moving boxes that still takes up most of the living area up there. Actually, it's a lovely apartment . . . or will be when I finally unpack."

"Well, at least you won't have a long drive home," Molly said. "I have the same situation at Bread on Arrival, and it's very convenient."

"It was part of the draw when I bought this house." Ed gestured to an arched doorway. "If you're not browsing for anything in particular, I'd recommend starting up this way. Follow me."

Molly trailed him through the arched doorway, then through another room before reaching one filled with cardboard boxes and wooden crates. A few stacks of books surrounded an antique shop counter and equally vintage cash register. In the center of the room was a large table piled with books on stands.

Molly's gaze swept over the boxes. "Are those full of books?"

"I went to an estate sale and bought the late owner's whole book collection," he said, a hint of amusement in his voice. "Practically sight unseen. Now it's like opening presents from distant relatives. Some are marvelous, and some are rather disappointing. Case in point." He pulled a small statuette of a hula girl from a box. The tiny dancer wiggled as he set it on a shelf.

Molly chuckled. "One man's trash . . ."

"Indeed. These boxes are supposed to be all books, but I keep unearthing surprises. I shouldn't complain, though. I was lucky to find an estate sale this time of year, and I probably wouldn't have if Lochside Realty hadn't sold me this place."

Molly found that remark a little confusing, but brushed it off, eager to explore the shop. She left the owner to his unpacking and wandered through the maze of rooms. Clearly Ed hadn't done any remodeling on the old farmhouse beyond adding lots of shelves, and the effect was charming. Many of the rooms were small, and Molly would have appreciated them being a little bit brighter, though she could see the house had a lot of windows. During the shop's normal hours, the windows probably offered sufficient light for browsing and reading. On this rainy late afternoon in February, it made them almost spooky.

Molly walked around another corner and found herself in a medium-size room with windows facing the road. A lovely brick fireplace on one wall had a small gas insert that flickered pleasantly. The glow from the fire offered more light, as did what appeared to be vintage wall sconces. Slightly worn wing chairs clustered around the fire in a cozy, inviting way. Molly thought she'd love to spend some time there with a good book.

The room also included a mishmash of bookshelves, some barely above waist height while others held books well out of Molly's reach, though none of the shelves were actually floor to ceiling. Along the fireplace's thin mantel, a row of china cats all stared at Molly.

Edging away from their feline scrutiny, she walked over to peer out one of the large windows, wondering if the rain had let up. With the light behind her, the glare made the window nearly a mirror, so Molly had to lean close to make anything out.

To her absolute shock, what she saw was a man standing near the window and glaring at her, his face contorted with rage. In the gloom beyond the man, a huge, dark, hairy creature crept toward him, and Molly's stomach plummeted.

She slapped her hand against the glass and shouted, "Behind you! It's a bear!"

2

Molly spun and ran for the door, desperate to get help for the man outside. She ran into Ed Richardson in the hall, and he caught her by the shoulders.

"What's wrong?" he asked.

Molly pulled free, still determined to get to the man but unsure of the closest route to reach him. "There's a bear outside," she said. "And a man." She darted around the bookseller, moving toward the foyer . . . or at least that was where she thought she was going.

He followed her, though he didn't touch her again. "A balding man?" he asked. "Medium height? And was the bear all black?"

Molly froze, baffled by the amusement in his tone. "Yes."

"That was Myron Webster," he said. "And the bear was his dog, Bernie. He's a Newfoundland. In the poor light and the rain, I could see mistaking Bernie for a bear. He's definitely a big dog."

"It was a dog?" Molly said weakly as she struggled to reconcile what he was saying versus what she'd believed she had seen through the window. She'd been so sure. Then she reminded herself of how strange it would be to see a bear anywhere in Michigan's UP in February when they should be tucked away hibernating.

"Yes, ma'am." Ed smiled slightly. "Myron walks Bernie by the shop a couple times a day so he can glare at me. I don't know why my bookshop works him up so much, but I'm sure that was Myron you saw."

As soon as the words were out of his mouth, Carol popped out of a doorway down the hall and hurried toward them. "Molly, did I hear you shouting?" She raised an eyebrow at Ed. "You should post maps around this place. All the little rooms are confusing."

"I'll consider that," he said agreeably.

"It was a false alarm." Molly could feel the heat rising in her cheeks about having been so wrong. "I thought I saw a bear outside."

Carol tapped a finger on her chin thoughtfully. "Well, that wouldn't be impossible, though not exactly likely in February. Unless the rain fooled it into thinking spring was here already."

"Maybe," the bookseller agreed, stretching the word into a drawl. "But in this case, I'm pretty sure it was Bernie."

"Bernie?" Carol echoed.

"A dog," Molly admitted.

"A huge dog," Edgar said supportively.

Molly waved away the effort to mitigate her mistake. "I feel foolish, so can we talk about something else? Did you find something for Maisie and Gavin?" Molly gestured toward the load of picture books tucked in Carol's arm.

"Oh yes." Carol showed them the stack of books one by one. Some of them Molly remembered from her own daughter's childhood, and she knew the seven-year-old twins would enjoy them. "I'm ready to check out." Carol gestured pointedly at Molly's empty hands. "Did you not find anything you wanted?"

"I got distracted by the false bear alarm and didn't do much shopping," Molly said. "But I enjoyed wandering around. This is a fascinating old house."

"Thank you," Ed said. "I feel the same way about it. Let me get you checked out." He led them to the room with the cardboard boxes.

Molly stood to one side as Carol paid for her books, but she hardly heard Carol's cheerful chatter about the fun classics she'd found. Molly was still feeling a little foolish about her mistake. *How could I have thought I was actually witnessing a bear attack?*

She was so deep in her own thoughts that she jumped when Carol squealed her name. Carol thrust both arms into one of the cardboard boxes and pulled out a life-size ceramic sculpture of a Scottish terrier. "This is adorable!" Carol gushed. "It could be Angus's twin, don't you think?"

Molly had seen the statue's head-tilted stance many times in her little dog. "It's certainly cute."

"You should buy it."

Carol thrust the dog into Molly's hands. The sculpture was a bit heavier than she'd expected. Molly wondered if that was a sign of a better piece of ceramic, one that was poured heavy in the mold. Of course, a life-size dog sculpture probably should have some heft to it. Now that she held it closer, the painted eyes seemed to beg for her attention. "I'm not sure I need two begging Scotties in my life."

"You could use it for a doorstop," Ed suggested. "You'd be doing me a favor by taking it off my hands since it's another of the unexpected bonus items from that estate sale." He waved a hand around. "I don't have the shelf space for it."

Molly laughed. "I'm not sure I do either."

"It would be adorable sitting next to the fireplace at the bakehouse," Carol said. "You could tie a bandana around its neck. Customers would love it."

Molly realized Carol's idea was a good one. Patrons would probably enjoy the little dog, and since Angus couldn't hang out in the bakery, it would be a nice tribute to him. "You're probably right, though I'm not sure I have a scarf that will work. It should be plaid, I think," Molly said. "A nice Highland tartan."

"Tartan would be perfect," Carol agreed.

Molly set the dog on the counter and patted its head before pulling out her credit card. "I'll take it."

"Excellent." Ed suggested a price that was more than reasonable, reassuring Molly that she'd made the right decision. After he'd rung up her purchase, he glanced at her. "If you don't mind, I'd like to add you to our e-mail list. That way you'll get notices of any specials." He picked up a pen and held it over his copy of the receipt, then peered at her expectantly.

"I gave him mine," Carol said.

"Sure." Molly told him her e-mail address, and he wrote it down along with her name and the word *bakery*, probably to help him remember her.

"Do you want me to wrap the dog?" Ed asked as he put the receipt in his cashbox and reached under the counter for paper.

"No, I can carry him." Molly had to admit she was already getting attached to the dog. It must be the strong resemblance to Angus. "And I promise I'll be back to buy books soon."

"You do that," Ed said. "In the meantime, take this one on me." He held out a novel that he'd retrieved from under the counter. "I finished reading it about an hour ago, and I think it's the perfect companion for the little dog. If you enjoy it, I have a few more in the series."

Molly flipped the book over in her hands. The cover was worn and slightly faded. but it featured a smiling man. "What's it about?"

"It's a mystery," Ed said. "You seemed like someone who would enjoy a good whodunit."

"She does," Carol assured him.

Molly raised an eyebrow. "As if you don't?"

"I'll read it after you," Carol offered. "If it's good."

"It is," Ed assured them as he slipped the book into a bag. "The main character plays the bagpipes, so he'd probably approve of this little dog."

"Perfect," Carol crowed. "Molly plays the bagpipes too."

Ed raised his thick eyebrows. "Now that I would never have pictured."

"She didn't say I played them well," Molly said. She nudged her friend. "And with that, we should be going. Harvey is going to tell you not to hang out with me anymore if you don't get home and feed him soon."

"Oh please," Carol said with a flap of her hand. "Harvey is perfectly capable of feeding himself. But I am starting to get a little hungry."

Once again, the bookseller thanked them for coming in and wished them a safe drive home. Molly tucked the book into her purse and hefted the Scottie into her arms before following Carol out into the darkness. To Molly's surprise, the icy drizzle they'd arrived with had become snowflakes.

"Oh no." Carol frowned up at the sky. "I hope the road doesn't get too slick." Then she snorted. "I used to make fun of people who fretted about driving in the snow, and now I've become one of them."

"You and me both."

The women walked carefully to the car. The snow had not yet begun to stick, and the steps and pavement didn't feel slippery under Molly's feet. She was glad for that, as she had had enough embarrassment for one evening without wiping out in a new business's parking lot.

As they approached Carol's car, Molly was startled by movement in her peripheral vision. To her surprise, she saw the same man who'd glared at her through the window, Myron Webster. As Ed had said, the man had a huge dog beside him. Molly felt a fresh wave of embarrassment that she'd confused the shaggy canine with a bear.

"Evening, ladies," Myron said. The smile he offered with his tip of the head transformed his face. He no longer seemed as dangerous as he had when Molly spotted him through the window. Now he was clearly a pleasant, middle-aged man with a dog.

"Evening," Molly said, tipping her own head.

"What a beautiful dog," Carol said, her tone almost teasing. "He reminds me of a bear."

"A teddy bear maybe." Myron reached out to pat the dog's head. "Isn't that right, Bernie?"

Bernie wagged his tail at the attention.

"You ladies drive carefully now," Myron said. "I heard the snow is only going to pick up."

"Thanks. Have a nice evening," Carol said as she hurried on to the car.

Molly followed her, but continued to sneak peeks at Myron and Bernie. The man had turned to stare at the farmhouse so Molly couldn't see his face, but his tense stance suggested he might be scowling again. *What an odd man.*

"Molly?" Carol asked, breaking into her thoughts. She already had the driver's side door open. "Are you coming?"

"Sorry." Molly hurried to get into the car. "Woolgathering."

"I thought that was *my* hobby," Carol said with a laugh.

As she drove, Carol leaned close to the window again, though her concern for the driving conditions didn't affect her willingness to chat. "I can completely understand why Beverly called me about that book. I've never seen another one that covered Fair Isle knitting so comprehensively. It not only has patterns, but stories behind the designs."

"Beverly made the find of the week, it seems," Molly said.

"She sure did," Carol agreed. "Her next order at the bakehouse is on me."

Molly didn't linger when Carol pulled up in front of Bread on Arrival. She knew her friend wanted to get home, so she hopped out with the dog statue in her arms. It took some juggling to get the front door open, but Molly managed it without dropping her new purchase.

She eyed the fireplace in the darkened bakery, wondering if she should leave the statue there. However, she didn't want to unveil it until she found a little scarf for its neck, so she decided to keep it upstairs in her apartment until then.

She passed through the bakehouse without flipping on any lights. One bonus of living upstairs was that no one knew the building better than she did. She'd walked through the downstairs rooms in the dark more than once. By the time she reached the steps, she knew Angus had heard her since he was barking from inside the apartment.

"I'm coming," she sang out and the barks stopped.

She shifted the hefty dog statue to one arm as she opened the door. Angus danced around her feet, clearly glad to have her home.

"I love you too," Molly assured the little dog, "but we'll both be happier if you don't trip me." Angus retreated a few feet, then resumed his excited prancing. Molly set the statue down on the apartment floor so she could shrug out of her jacket and hang it up.

At the sight of the statue, Angus stopped his welcome-home ritual and sniffed the imitation dog before growling deep in his throat.

"It's okay, Angus," Molly said. "It's only a decoration."

Angus didn't even glance at her. He'd locked eyes with the statue and continued to growl as the hair rose on his back. Molly worried that Angus would try attacking the statue—that could lead to one or both being damaged, so she scooped the statue up again. Apparently a spot downstairs near the fireplace, where Angus rarely went, was the safest place for the newcomer.

Molly walked to the nearest closet and quickly settled the statue on the top shelf. *I'll get it down when I find a scarf for it, maybe sometime when Angus is out in the yard.*

As soon as she closed the door, Angus stopped growling, though he eyed the closet door with some suspicion.

"It's okay," she told him. "Let's go get some supper." That grabbed Angus's full attention. He dashed for the kitchen, leaving Molly chuckling as she followed in his wake. She dropped her purse off on one of the kitchen chairs and felt a thrill when she caught sight of the book tucked inside. *Oh, that's right. A new book!*

After Molly and Angus finished their supper and took a quick walk in the falling snow, they settled together on the sofa. Pressed against Molly's side, Angus gave a deep sigh and was asleep within a minute. Molly opened the book with a smile. A cozy seat, a warm puppy, and a new mystery series—how could life get any better? Molly was soon completely engrossed in the exploits of the bagpipe-playing detective and read far later into the night than she should have. *I'll feel that in the morning*, she thought when she finally headed off to bed. *But it was worth it.*

Tuesday morning broke with the promise of better weather, or at least that was how it seemed to Molly as she peeked out her bedroom window at the crystalline blue skies above Loch Mallaig, the town's namesake lake. Molly had overslept a little and by the time she was ready to head downstairs, she already heard sounds of movement. Carol and Laura had beaten her to work.

When Molly walked into the bakehouse kitchen, her partners aimed almost identical grins at her. "Morning, sleepyhead," Carol said. "Up late reading?"

Molly gaped at her in surprise. "How did you know?"

Her friends both laughed. "We've all fallen hard for new novels before," Laura said. "And Carol told me the one you got from the bookstore sounded like a winner."

"A bagpipe-playing detective?" Carol grinned. "How much more on the nose can a book get?"

"Adair Abernathy, the main character in the book, plays much better than I do," Molly said as she began prepping the shipping area. With Valentine's Day close, she knew packing mail orders would be nearly a full-time task. Bread on Arrival sold a surprising amount online, especially around the holidays, and Carol's decorated cookies were particularly popular right now. "And he's a detective, which I am not."

"Sure you're not," Carol agreed pleasantly.

Molly narrowed her eyes. She suspected she was being teased, but her friend's face was the picture of innocence.

"I still need to frost the next batch of cookies and let them set, so you don't have anything to pack yet," Carol said.

"I'll stock the front displays then." Although not as talented in the kitchen as Carol and Laura, Molly happily filled in wherever needed in the bakehouse. Her greatest gifts came in marketing and publicity, but she also handled much of the office work. She didn't mind that her skills as a baker weren't often called upon since her friends never let her doubt the importance of her contributions.

By the time Bridget arrived to open, Molly had all the front displays full again. "How was your class?" she asked.

"Terrific," Bridget told her with wide-eyed enthusiasm. "My professor is amazing, even if he is kind of cranky. Some of my friends are amazed that I'm not intimidated by the man's growling, but I work with Hamish Bruce. I am not easily cowed."

"Good for you!" Like Bridget, Hamish worked part-time, but the two couldn't have been more different. Where Bridget was enthusiastic about everything, Hamish was a proud curmudgeon who never saw a situation that didn't warrant at least a little grumbling. The one trait they both shared was absolute loyalty to their friends, and Molly appreciated them tremendously.

Movement outside the front window drew Molly's attention, and she saw two Loch Mallaig police officers heading for the bakery door. Since the sign on the door was still flipped to *Closed*, Molly expected the police officers to simply stand and chat as they waited for the bakery to open. Instead, there was a firm rap on the doorframe.

Bridget spun around to face the door. "Someone's here early."

"It's two police officers," Molly said. "And I'm pretty sure one of them is Greer Anderson. You'd best let them in."

"Police officers?" Bridget raised her dark brows before heading to the door to let them in.

Greer Anderson entered first, followed by another officer that Molly recognized as well, Michael Drummond. In her early thirties, Greer was substantially younger than Molly, but they'd become friendly, mostly from their time in the local bagpiping group The Piping Yoopers.

Although short and blonde like Molly, Greer had a more athletic build and a steady nature. Officer Drummond wasn't easy to rattle either. He was a few years older than Greer, nearing forty in fact, with the fair skin and dark red hair that was common in Loch Mallaig.

"Good morning." Molly noted the professional way both of them scanned the room. "What brings you by so early?"

"Molly," Greer said. "We need to speak to you and Carol."

"Is something wrong?" Molly asked, a sudden tightness in her chest. For an instant, her mind flashed to her daughter. *Is Chloe all right?* But then reason pushed the idea aside. They wouldn't want to talk to Carol if it involved Chloe.

"It would be best if we spoke to you and Carol at the same time so we don't need to repeat ourselves." Greer's voice was professional and serious. Molly found her tone disconcerting, since she and the officer had shared coffee and laughter together here in the bakery so many times.

"I'll get Carol," Bridget offered before practically running for the kitchen.

"I'm happy to speak to you about whatever you need," Molly said. "But can you give me some idea of what's wrong?" If they weren't in the building right now, Molly would think there must be some problem with the bakehouse, but that didn't make any sense. With all the logical guesses discarded, Molly felt completely clueless.

Carol walked into the front room and Molly caught sight of Laura lingering in the doorway leading toward the kitchen. "Can I help you?" Carol asked.

"Were you and Molly at Books & Bargains last night?" Greer asked.

"Yes," Carol said. "We went right after work so I could buy a knitting book."

"Has something happened to the shop?" For some odd reason, the image of the scowling man and the bear that Molly had seen through a window came back to her. But she knew what she'd seen wasn't a bear. What was going on?

"The owner, Edgar Richardson," Greer said. "Did you see him?"

"Yes, of course," Carol answered. "He sold me the book. He seems nice."

"He was unpacking boxes from an estate sale," Molly volunteered, though she felt silly immediately after saying it. What difference could that make? "Is he all right?"

For an instant, Greer's professional demeanor broke and her expression grew sad. "No, I'm afraid not. Edgar Richardson is dead."

Molly thought of the genial bookseller and felt her eyes fill with mournful tears. He was so nice. At a guess, she would have put him around seventy, but he certainly hadn't appeared sick or frail, though maybe a little thin. "He seemed okay when we spoke with him. Was it a heart attack or something?"

"No." Officer Drummond gazed solemnly at them. "We can't be altogether sure, but the signs point to murder."

3

"Murder?" Molly repeated, her voice thin as she wrapped her arms around herself. She was completely stunned, though she couldn't say exactly why this hit her so hard. Maybe it was the fact that she'd left the bookstore firmly intending to visit again and chat further with the owner. Her meeting with him had felt like a beginning, not an end.

"Why?" Carol asked, her own voice stronger and without the tremor Molly heard in her own. "What happened?"

"We're actually here to ask you questions," Drummond said drily. "But we can't answer that anyway. Cause of death is still undetermined."

"Then what makes you think it was murder?" Molly asked.

"The store was trashed," Greer said. "Clearly someone was hunting for something. The search was especially thorough around the cash register, which was where the man's body was found. The apartment had been ransacked as well."

"So they must not have been looking for a book," Carol suggested. "Otherwise they would have gone through all the rooms."

"Or they found it before needing to extend the search," Greer said.

"What could someone have wanted from a used bookstore?" Molly asked.

"Valuables?" Officer Drummond suggested. "I'm told that first editions can be extremely expensive."

"He did have some older books," Molly said. "In fact, he said the books on the top shelves of the foyer were old and in need of repair. Maybe some of them were first editions."

The officer scribbled a note on his pad before peering at her again. "Did he mention any other specific valuables?"

Molly shook her head. "No, and it would have been hard to tell which items in his collection had value. There wasn't much organization yet, but he hadn't been open very long. That brings us again to Carol's point. Why wouldn't the mess be the same in every room? That bookshop was a maze of halls and rooms, and all of them had shelves and books."

"Good questions," Greer said. She smiled, her expression slightly impish. "And while you're offering us suggestions about the case, do you suppose we could sit down and have some coffee?"

Carol's eyes widened as if she was startled by her own lack of hospitality. "Of course. Let me get a few cups. We just made a pot."

Carol headed for the counter area while Molly gestured toward a café table. Officer Drummond grabbed two chairs from another table and hauled them over.

As soon as they were seated and Carol returned with coffee, Greer put her notebook on the table and flipped pages. "Now that we've done what we could for your curiosity, maybe you could both answer a couple questions for us." She gazed at them expectantly.

"Of course," Carol answered and Molly added her murmur of agreement.

"What time did you arrive at the bookstore?" Greer asked.

"It's hard to say exactly," Molly said. "Between four and five."

Carol nodded agreement. "We had closed up here, and Molly settled Angus upstairs before we left. The weather was disgusting, so I drove slowly, but it's not terribly far, of course. It was probably closer to five."

"Sounds right," Molly agreed.

"Did you see anything or anyone suspicious when you arrived?" Greer asked.

"We were the only ones in the parking lot," Molly said. "The rain made it tough to see clearly. Plus, we were focused on getting inside."

"That's true," Carol chimed in. "Bigfoot could have been watching from the tree line, and I wouldn't have noticed. I was on a mission to pick up a knitting book."

Officer Drummond raised his pen from the pad. "Was the book all you bought?"

"No," Carol said. "I got a pile of books for my grandkids, and Molly bought a dog."

That was met with surprise from both officers. "Edgar Richardson was selling dogs from his bookstore?" Officer Drummond asked at the same time that Greer blurted, "Angus isn't enough?"

Molly held up a hand. "It was a Scottie dog statue. About this big." She gestured with her hands. "And Angus is not a fan. I'm planning to put it down here next to the fire after I find a scarf for it. Right now it's in the closet where it can't start a dogfight."

Greer exchanged a glance with the other officer. "That explains the witness report."

"Witness report?" Molly and Carol repeated together, their voices equally surprised.

"A neighbor reported seeing two women with their arms full of something hurrying from the building," Greer said. "He thought you were burglars."

That brought a bark of laughter from Carol. "Was this the man with the dog?"

"If you can call that thing a dog," Officer Drummond said. "I am fairly sure my daughter could ride it."

"Molly thought it was a bear when she saw it." Carol's tone was matter-of-fact with no hint that she thought the misidentification was silly, but Molly still winced.

"It was hard to see in the rain," Molly protested.

"Did either of you speak at length to the shop owner?" Greer asked.

"Only about the books," Carol said. "He was nice though."

"I chatted with him briefly," Molly said. "He was unpacking boxes from an estate sale and talked about how they were supposed to be filled with only books, but weren't. And he was the one who told me about his neighbor and the dog. I'm afraid I don't remember the neighbor's name, but I know the dog is Bernie."

"The neighbor is Myron Webster." Greer set her pen down to take a sip of her coffee. "Did Edgar Richardson mention having trouble with anyone?"

"Well, when he told me about Mr. Webster and the dog," Molly said, "he did mention that Mr. Webster would pass by several times a day to glare at the bookstore."

"Yeah," Drummond said as he slowly spun his coffee cup in his hands. "We noticed his hostility. Apparently he's upset about having a business in what is predominately a residential neighborhood."

"Doesn't seem like much of a motive to kill someone," Carol said.

Greer shook her head. "No, we're assuming the robbery is the key here. Though it's early, and we're open to new ideas. So other than the neighbor, did you see anyone else?"

"No," Molly said. "But I'm still shocked that anyone would kill such a nice man. Even in a burglary, couldn't they have easily done something other than kill the man? He was at least seventy. Surely murder wasn't necessary."

"Most people are nice to someone," Officer Drummond said. "That doesn't mean they don't have enemies."

"Actually," Greer cut in, "in this case, I suspect we'll find the strain of dealing with the burglar brought on a heart attack or something similar. He was, as Molly said, not a young man. If that is what happened, the most we'll be able to do is tack on a manslaughter charge to the burglary. I doubt it will stick, though."

"But you're sure it was a burglary?" Carol asked. "The mess wasn't there to confuse you about the murder?"

Greer laughed. "Most criminals aren't that bright. The cashbox was open and empty. Plus, there was some sign of struggle, or at least anger on the part of the burglar."

"Anger?" Molly echoed.

"Smashed curios. I think it was a fit of temper over not getting more loot." Greer held up a finger. "But we are considering all possibilities, as I said."

With their coffee finished and their questions asked, the two officers thanked Molly and Carol for their time and left. "Let us know if you think of anything else," Greer said as she went out the door.

Molly agreed they would. The moment the door was closed on the two officers, Laura and Bridget rushed into the room.

"A murder!" Bridget exclaimed. "How do you guys keep running into these things?"

"That's a question I ask myself frequently." Molly looked from Bridget to Laura. "You heard everything?"

"I did," Laura said. "And I think we're going to have to be ready for a crowd today. Once it gets around that you two were at the scene of a murder, we're going to get as many information seekers as pastry lovers. I think you both had best stay away from the customers today, for the sake of your sanity."

"I won't argue," Molly said. "I am feeling so sad about this. I liked the man, and I think he would have fit in to this town well."

"Things like this remind me of how fragile we all are," Carol admitted. "We need to appreciate every day we get."

"And on that cheery note," Laura said. "I've got baking to do."

"Sounds good," Carol said. "Baking soothes."

Molly patted Bridget on the arm. "Are you feeling up to the deluge?"

Bridget beamed at her. "Bring 'em on."

Molly felt sure Bridget would handle the customers with ease, but Laura called in Hamish to give her a hand anyway. No one dared push too much with the retired history teacher around. He had no problem saying exactly what he thought at any given moment, even to a customer. Sometimes Molly winced at Hamish's bluntness, but she couldn't argue that he'd be the perfect counterpoint to Bridget's friendly deflection.

As Molly settled into the task of packing up Valentine's Day treats, she found the repetitiveness soothing. Plus, the attention required to make each package secure and attractive helped keep her imagination from taking her down unhelpful roads. Still, even the big stack of orders was eventually packed and ready for pickup. Molly had some computer work she could do upstairs, but she decided to take Angus for a walk first.

"I'll be up in the office when I get back," she told Carol and Laura. She patted her pocket. "I have my phone if you need me."

"Have a nice walk," Carol said as she dusted her table with flour before rolling out sugar cookies. "But be careful. There were slippery spots when I walked in. The weather cannot figure out if we should stick with winter or flirt with early spring."

"I'll vote for early spring," Laura said. "Though I have to admit, the temperature here in the kitchen always feels so much nicer in winter."

Before she headed upstairs to collect Angus, Molly peeked through the doorway at the front customer area. She saw a slender man in need of a shave peering at Bridget. "Are you Molly or Carol?" he asked.

"She's neither," Hamish told the man shortly. "What kind of pastry do you want today?"

The man glared at Hamish as if he were thinking about arguing, but few people had that kind of nerve. Ultimately he simply asked for a bagel. A smile tugged at the corners of Molly's mouth as she headed toward the stairs. It was clear the customers were in good hands.

Molly hoped the walk would help cheer her up. The sight of Angus in his jaunty red winter jacket rarely failed to cheer her. Plus, she loved Loch Mallaig, even in the thick of winter. The snow softened the edges of all the buildings and gave the landscape the beauty of a Christmas card.

Unfortunately, today the damp cold and gray skies seemed to reflect the gloom she was having trouble shaking.

"At least the sidewalks are clear," she told Angus. He glanced up at her briefly before returning to sniffing a clump of dirt peeking out from under a patch of snow. Angus had a tendency to take personal offense whenever the snow on the sidewalk was higher than his short legs, so Molly knew he appreciated the clear pavement. As Carol had warned, Molly did find patches of ice wherever the sidewalk was in deep shade. The care necessary to keep her footing helped distract her from thoughts of the murder.

When Angus stopped again for a good sniff, Molly idly scanned the area. When her gaze fell on the bakehouse, she saw the slender man with the beard step out into the feeble February sunlight. Seen from a distance, the man appeared even thinner and more than a little scruffy. Molly thought he would do well to eat as many bagels as possible. *It is possible to be too thin.*

For some reason, that thought brought her an image of the long-legged bookstore owner. *Who would want to hurt that nice man?* She knew better than most that it was nearly impossible to truly know someone. Though Carol and Laura were like sisters to Molly, most of the rest of Loch Mallaig was still open to discovery. For example, she was quite certain she'd never seen the thin man with the scruffy beard, though he'd come into the bakehouse with her name and Carol's on his lips.

She mused again about how quickly Hamish had shot down the thin man's question. Hamish was a case in point about the problem with first impressions. Sometimes the grumpiest people like him had the kindest hearts, and folks who seemed cheerful could be hiding dark secrets.

Was Ed Richardson in the latter category? She remembered him mentioning Detroit during the brief time they'd chatted, so he'd spent time living in the city. Urban life could have some rough edges. Molly wondered if he'd worked in a bookstore there or had some other kind of job. Could something from the city have followed him to Loch Mallaig?

For now, the whole situation held few answers, and Molly knew it would be best if she stayed out of it. But she wasn't exactly good at staying out of things, especially when they thrust themselves into her life. After all, what if she and Carol had been outside the bookshop as the killer was preparing to go in? Molly found herself wondering if the police knew a time of death. *I should have asked Greer.*

If there had been someone outside, Molly and Carol might not have seen the person. They'd been fairly focused on getting to the car and getting home. They hadn't seen any other cars, but if the burglar had parked down the road, Molly would never have noticed with the bad weather.

Molly's thoughts were interrupted as Angus suddenly stiffened near her feet and yipped. Molly glanced up, but saw no one ahead. Then she realized Angus's attention was on something behind her. At exactly that moment, a firm hand dropped onto her shoulder.

Molly shrieked.

4

Molly spun, her heart pounding so hard it almost hurt. Fergus MacGregor stepped back, holding up both hands. His handsome face was a picture of apology.

"I'm sorry, Molly," he said. "I didn't mean to scare you. I thought you'd gotten the heads-up from Angus." Fergus leaned down to pat the little dog on the head, a gesture that was well received by the Scottie.

Molly rested a hand on her chest, huffing slightly but mildly embarrassed at reacting so dramatically to a hand on her shoulder. "That's okay. I was lost in thought. No harm done."

His expression still sheepish, he straightened again. "I wanted to check on how you were faring after hearing you and Carol witnessed a murder last night. You should have called me. That must have been horrifying."

Molly gaped at him until he stopped speaking. "Carol and I didn't witness a murder. Where did you hear that?"

To Molly's further surprise, Fergus's cheeks darkened, visible even through his beard. He didn't blush often and since she seemed to blush a dozen times a day, she enjoyed the sight of someone else being discomforted for a change.

"I overheard some of the staff talking at Castleglen," he admitted. "I should have realized that local gossip might not be entirely true. I'm glad the report was wildly inflated. So what did happen?"

For an instant, Molly was distracted by the thought that most bosses of businesses as large as Castleglen wouldn't mix close enough with the staff to hear much local gossip. She couldn't even guess how many people were employed at the golf resort and lodge with its gift shop, spa, fitness center, and two restaurants. Of course, Fergus had grown up in the place, which had been owned by his family since it was opened in 1951, so mingling with staff wasn't a strange concept for him.

"There *was* a murder," Molly admitted. "Or the police think it could be murder. It might have been a burglary that brought on the man's death by natural causes. It's all a bit up in the air at the moment, but Carol and I weren't witnesses to it. We simply went shopping at Books & Bargains and spoke to the owner. Unfortunately, he died after we left. Granted, that part has me reeling a little. He was a nice man."

"That's the new bookstore at the edge of town, right?" Fergus asked tentatively, clearly unsure of any of his information. When Molly nodded, he went on, "I hadn't met him, though I planned to visit the shop sometime. I heard the police spoke to you both. Was that part true?"

"Greer Anderson and Michael Drummond came to the bakehouse this morning. They were nice, but it's still disconcerting to be questioned in a criminal investigation. And this has hit me hard. I was looking forward to revisiting the bookstore and maybe becoming friends with the owner. I think he would have fit in so well here in Loch Mallaig."

"Your kind heart reflects well on you, Molly." Fergus's expression filled with concern again. "You've probably only struck the tip of the iceberg on fielding questions about last night. I've already run into several people asking me about it simply because you and I are friends. That tells me you're going to be hit with some unwelcome attention, especially since the rumor mill isn't exactly accurate."

"We figured there would be people popping in at the bakery for the sole purpose of mining for gossip," Molly said. "Carol and I have been hiding out in the kitchen all morning. I only slipped out to walk

Angus and get some fresh air. I should probably be surprised that you're the only person who's stopped me so far." Molly's gaze swept the sidewalks around them. Early February wasn't exactly a boom time for downtown Loch Mallaig, and the streets were mostly quiet. Normally Molly loved the town in winter, when the deep quiet of winter made everything snug and cozy, and when she knew almost everyone she met.

As she scanned the area, Molly spotted someone she definitely recognized—a balding man and a huge, black dog coming toward them on the other side of the street. The shaggy dog ambled along, pausing only for the occasional sniff.

"I know him," Molly said, gesturing toward the pair. "He is the neighbor of the bookstore owner. Carol and I spoke to him briefly last night in the parking lot."

Fergus followed her gaze. "An interesting coincidence. I'm fairly sure I haven't spotted that pair before. I think I'd remember since that is easily the biggest dog I've ever seen."

Myron Webster must have recognized Molly because he raised a hand and crossed the street. As he was jaywalking in the middle of a block, Molly was concerned to see he didn't even check for traffic before heading across at a brisk pace. The dog lingered where he was for a moment before catching up to his owner with clear reluctance.

"Mr. Webster," Molly said as soon as he was within earshot. "You should be more careful of cars."

"Oh." The man squinted at the street. "I suppose I should. I was so surprised to see you, and I wanted to speak to you."

As soon as he reached them, Angus strained at the end of his leash to reach the big dog. Bernie snuffled the little Scottie in a friendly, if rather overbearing way. The wagging tails on both dogs suggested this was the beginning of a fast friendship.

"Mr. Webster," Molly said. "This is my friend, Fergus MacGregor."

Fergus nodded and gave a welcoming smile. "How do you do? That's an impressive dog you have there. What breed is it?"

"A Newfoundland," the man said. "Bernie was a rescue. Apparently his original owners had no idea that Newfoundlands grew so large. Why would anyone buy a puppy with no understanding of the dog it will grow into?"

"I have no idea," Fergus said.

The other man shook his head in disapproval. "Some people so casually make decisions with no thought to the consequences."

"Clearly Bernie is lucky to have you now," Fergus said.

"I'm the lucky one in this pairing," Myron said. "Bernie is a perfect Michigan dog. He isn't bothered by the cold. I figure if I ever keel over in the snow, Bernie will haul me home."

"That's something Angus certainly couldn't manage," Molly said. "By the way, I don't believe I introduced myself last night. I'm Molly Ferris."

"I'm Myron Webster." He shifted nervously for a moment before patting his dog on the head. "Bernie and I don't usually come into town. He doesn't see so well and can be frightened by strange sounds, but I knew there wouldn't be many people out in the cold. I planned to come by the bakery and speak to you."

Molly raised her eyebrows. "Speak to me?"

"You and your friend," Myron said. "I wanted to say that I hoped I didn't cause either of you any trouble with the police by mentioning the two of you. They asked me about seeing anyone around the bookstore, and you were the only people I'd seen."

"You didn't cause us any trouble," Molly assured him. "Carol and I are happy to help the police in any way possible. It's always a good idea to tell the truth. But how did you know we owned Bread on Arrival?"

The man smiled. "Oh, I have visited your place a number of times. I enjoy the melting moments very much. You could say those cookies are my guilty pleasure. You probably don't remember me since I don't usually come in with Bernie here." He patted the dog again. "Of the two of us, Bernie makes the greatest impression by far. I'm rather ordinary."

"There is nothing wrong with being ordinary," Fergus said. "It works for me."

Myron's expression darkened a bit when he studied Fergus, and Molly figured Myron suspected Fergus was being condescending. Molly knew that wasn't the case. Fergus was handsome, but he considered himself quite ordinary. It was one of the things she appreciated about him.

"You're welcome to bring Bernie to the bakehouse next time since Angus here is happy to host other dogs in our fenced-in yard," Molly said to shift the subject to safer ground. "And I will pass your cookie compliments on to Carol and Laura. They're the ones who do the bulk of the baking." Molly wondered how best to ask the man about his antipathy toward the bookstore, but he spoke before she could decide on her best course of action.

"I'm so glad I came to town today," Myron said. "I've been fretting about the conversation with the police, and now you've put me completely at ease."

"Molly is good at putting people at ease," Fergus said. "And I've never known her to hold a grudge."

"Excellent traits," Myron said as Bernie flopped down on the pavement, bumping into Myron's leg as he did so. The weight of the big dog made the man stumble a bit, but he caught himself right away. Molly almost laughed when Angus lay down nose to nose with the massive dog.

"I believe Angus and Bernie have become buddies," Fergus said.

"Good," Molly replied. Then she decided to simply dive into the topic she wanted to discuss. "I imagine the police must have been happy to talk with you, Myron. You must have seen the comings and goings at the bookstore quite a bit. The owner told me that you walk Bernie by the shop frequently."

Myron's smile faded. "Well, the shop is right next to my house. Of course I'd take Bernie by there. A big dog like this needs frequent walks. Otherwise he'd gain too much weight, which can lead to joint strain and other health problems." He waved a hand toward Angus. "I'm pleased to see your own dog is so trim."

"Yes, Angus gets a lot of exercise," Molly replied. She suspected she'd offended the man somehow but wasn't completely certain how. She was beginning to realize Myron was probably not the easiest person to be around.

"Did the bookstore bring a lot of traffic to the street?" Fergus asked, pulling the man's attention from Molly, much to her relief.

Myron snorted. "Hardly. In fact, I expect that shop was going to be a total flop." He turned to Molly again. "You were inside. You must have seen what a maze that place is. Who would put up with that in a shop? You'd never find anything."

"It did mean he could have a lot of cozy nooks." Molly felt slightly defensive, especially since the bookstore hadn't gotten much of a chance to thrive.

"I suppose," Myron said, though his tone suggested anything but agreement. "I am sorry something dreadful happened to Ed Richardson, but I won't pretend that I'm going to miss that shop. I am not interested in seeing our residential neighborhood become commercial. We are close enough to the businesses in town without having them creeping down our street."

"I can see that," Fergus said agreeably. "I probably wouldn't want to see a shop open next to my house either."

Molly had no comment to that, since she lived in a shop. She knew what Myron said was reasonable enough, but there was something about the man's delivery that seemed practiced. She was certain his antagonism toward the bookstore was real enough, but Molly questioned whether it really had anything to do with the spread of the business district. Myron Webster struck her as angry, maybe chronically angry . . . but why?

5

Molly woke well before her alarm went off the next morning. As she sat up in the dark bedroom, she had the uncomfortable feeling of bursting from a bad dream whose tattered images were fading fast. With a shudder, she shoved her feet into her slippers and shuffled to the bathroom for a shower. Sometimes sleep was less a refuge and more an arena where worries battered the sleeper all through the night.

With her early rising she was able to walk Angus and get to the bakery kitchen before either Carol or Laura had arrived. The brisk cold of the walk had helped dispel any lingering weariness from the tough night. Though Molly wasn't comfortable starting any of the day's breads or pastries, she got the coffee going and checked over the daily and weekly to-do lists so she could do some prep for her friends, like pulling butter out of the cooler to soften.

Laura and Carol constantly encouraged Molly to tackle baking projects outside her comfort zone, and she did occasionally try her hand at something new. But overall she was happy with her spot as a backup baker. Besides, that freed her to maintain the website, plan promotions, and generally do much of her work behind the scenes. In fact, their current *Love is in the Air* promotion was her brainchild and had brought many new customers in to purchase Valentine's treats.

"Either that or they came to gawk at Carol and me," Molly muttered as she finished unwrapping sticks of butter and piling them into a stainless steel bowl. Yesterday afternoon had been crazy busy and they'd sold a massive amount of heart-shaped cookies and pastries, but Bridget had also reported that she and Hamish had dealt with many busybodies during the shop hours. Molly couldn't help being impressed by the efficiency of the Loch Mallaig gossip network.

With a sigh, Molly walked out to the front of the bakery to check over the room and make sure it was clean. Beyond the front windows, the street was still dark with golden pools of illumination offered by streetlights. Molly gazed out at the darkness and wondered again about the bookseller's death. She hoped the police would solve the crime soon. Surely that would help her stop dwelling on it.

Sounds from the back drew her into the kitchen, where she found Carol bustling around. "Good morning," Molly said.

Carol glanced up with a smile. "You're an early bird today. We both even beat Laura."

"I couldn't get back to sleep so I figured I'd be productive. How are you this morning?"

"A little ragged," Carol said. "I didn't sleep well, which is why I'm here early too. And I could have done without Harvey reading me newspaper blurbs about the burglary and the death of that poor man."

Molly shuddered. "I have avoided the news specifically because I didn't want to think about it more than I already am."

"Lucky you." Carol picked up the to-do list for the day and scanned it before continuing. "Harvey did find out that Edgar Richardson was a retired police detective from Detroit. I thought that was interesting."

Molly blinked. "Really? I knew he was from Detroit, but I would never have pictured him as a big city police detective. I wonder if that had anything to do with his death. I imagine someone in that line of work would have enemies."

"The newspaper Harvey was reading me hinted at that. Apparently the police are expanding their investigation to examine the man's last cases."

Molly wrapped her arms around herself. "Does it make me a bad person if I hope it *is* someone associated with his work in Detroit instead of anyone from around here?"

"I imagine it makes you like the rest of us." Carol picked up the bowl of butter Molly had left on the table. "Would you mind cutting three sticks of this into cubes?" She showed the size with her fingers. "That will help me get moving on cookies. With Valentine's Day on Saturday, we'll need a lot of the iced shortbread hearts."

Molly grabbed the bowl. "I'm on it." She was almost able to forget about murder and mayhem while she cubed butter and did other prep jobs as directed by Carol, then Laura when she arrived a short time later.

When Bridget sailed in to open for the day, she beamed her usual sunny smile to everyone. "Will Hamish be in today?"

"Yes, but not for a couple of hours yet," Laura replied, her hands deep in a bowl of bread dough.

"I'll come out and help with the initial rush," Molly offered when she saw Bridget's slightly alarmed expression in response to Laura's news.

Bridget immediately became sunny again. "Thank you. Yesterday was a zoo. I can't imagine handling it alone. Though I'm not sure you'll be as good at quelling the unruly as Hamish is."

"No one is as good at quelling the unruly as Hamish is," Carol offered, making the others laugh.

Molly soon had cause to miss Hamish as they faced a rush of customers who craved gossip as much as Selkirk Bannocks and oatcakes. Molly thought her biggest shock was when the tiny, birdlike Mrs. Gaddie asked if she'd gotten any of the murdered man's blood on her and whether she'd show them if she did.

"I didn't see any murdered men," she assured the elderly woman as firmly as she could manage. "When I met Mr. Richardson, he wasn't bleeding. He was unpacking boxes."

The woman appeared so disappointed that Molly almost felt sorry for her.

The next person in line was far less inquisitive. It was the Bakehouse Three's friend, Beverly Scott. As always, the real estate agent was impeccably dressed in a stylishly-cut dark suit and heels. Molly wondered briefly how she managed in those shoes on the icy streets.

Beverly's dark eyes filled with sympathy as she said, "I came to pick up the melting moments for my open house."

"It's unusual to have an open house in the middle of the week, isn't it?" Molly asked.

"I moved it up," Beverly said. "The weather reports for the weekend are ominous. And I want to get it over with before there's any more talk about a wave of burglaries heading for Loch Mallaig. That doesn't exactly help with a home sale."

"A wave?" Molly echoed.

Beverly nodded. "I assume you didn't see the *Crown Press News* yet today. They're spreading some balderdash that a team of burglars are targeting Loch Mallaig, and that's how the poor bookstore owner was killed." Her expression saddened. "He was a nice man."

"I thought so too," Molly said. "But I hadn't heard about a team of burglars." Certainly Officers Anderson and Drummond hadn't mentioned such a thing, though they had said the shop had been ransacked. But where had the *team* idea come from?

"It's in the paper," a man called from behind Beverly. "A pair of violent home invaders. And women to boot. They marched out of the shop bold as brass with armloads of loot and a dead man in their wake."

"The newspaper report didn't say home invaders," Beverly insisted, but she was soon drowned out by other contributions called from around the bakery.

Mrs. Gaddie rushed back to the counter. "Are we all going to wake up to find out we've been murdered in our sleep?"

"I don't think that's even possible," Molly replied and she heard a definite snicker from Bridget behind her. More shouts answered that, and Molly wasn't sure what to do in response to the growing mob. Then she heard a voice she recognized well.

"What is wrong with you people?"

Every eye turned to Grizela Duff, the head librarian at the Loch Mallaig Library. She stood just inside the front door with her hands on her ample hips, her elbows jutting sharply out like weapons. "This is a bakery, not a press conference," Grizela continued, her normally stern voice sharp as a razor. "Why are you bothering these women with your foolishness?"

"We're not bothering anyone," Mrs. Gaddie said sullenly, but she scurried away from the counter and took a seat at one of the tables, casting baleful glances at Grizela as she went. The rest of the customers didn't even have the nerve to offer that much resistance. Instead, they straightened their line at the counter and studied their toes.

"Good," Grizela said, though she still sounded anything but pleased. "Now can we conduct ourselves like adults? I have a cake to pick up."

No one answered, but from then on the customers stuck to the topic of their orders. None of them appeared happy about it, but no one had the nerve to cross the intimidating librarian. By the time Grizela reached the counter to pick up her cake, Hamish had arrived to take over for Molly.

Molly headed to the kitchen and stopped at the table where Carol was carefully icing heart-shaped cookies. "Did Harvey read you any articles about a team of burglars in Loch Mallaig?"

"No." Carol frowned. "What an odd idea."

"Apparently it was in the *Crown Press News*."

Carol made a disgusted noise. "Harvey reads the *Crown Press News* in order to make fun of them. He says it's gossip in its purest form. Was it in today's paper? I left before it arrived."

"Yep. It seems to me that Greer would have said something if the police thought there was a team of burglars," Molly said. "Maybe I can find the article online."

"I'd be curious to hear it," Carol agreed.

"Me too," Laura put in from across the room at an industrial mixer. "If there is a team of burglars, I want to know. My cottage isn't exactly full of antiques, but I have a few nice pieces. I'd hate to lose them." She assessed the dough in the giant metal bowl. "This will keep me busy for a little bit, but we'll read it as soon as we have a break. For now, Molly, do you think you could start packing mail orders? The icing on the batch of cookies Carol did earlier has set, so they can be boxed."

"I'm on it." Molly was burning with curiosity about the newspaper report, but when Laura was in production mode, it was best to follow her lead. And the job of filling orders was soothing. No one demanded answers from her. She simply focused on carefully packing the boxes and affixing labels.

By late morning, Molly still hadn't had a chance to read the newspaper article. She finished preparing the day's shipments and headed out front to grab a cup of coffee as a reward. As she was pouring the cup, Officer Drummond reached the front of the line of customers and asked Bridget for a scone and a cup of coffee.

Molly walked over as Bridget slid the officer's scone into a bag to go. "Do you have a minute?" she asked him.

"Just about," he said. Then his attention sharpened. "Why? Did you think of something?"

"Maybe you could step into the kitchen?" Molly suggested. "I promise not to keep you long."

His hopeful expression became suspicious, but he followed Molly, sipping his coffee as he walked. "What can I help you with?"

"Can you tell us how the investigation is going?" Molly asked.

The officer harrumphed. "I should have known I'd be hit with an interrogation. Your excellent scones lured me in."

"Flattery will get you nowhere," Carol said from a nearby workstation, where she was slipping bread into wrappers. "Spill."

"I think we deserve to know," Molly said more gently. "We've been in the middle of the storm here. It seems everyone who comes in has heard some wild tale or other. Right now, the rumor is that there's a team of violent home invaders preying on the town."

"That's simply ridiculous." Drummond took a long sip of his coffee, clearly stalling for time. Then he sighed. "I shouldn't be commenting on an open investigation, but apparently everyone else is."

"Definitely," Molly said.

"Okay. I can say that our initial assessment about the murder could be wrong," he said. "Although clearly there was a burglary, it appears the victim died of a heart attack. We found no heart medication in his apartment, though, so if he had a bad heart, he wasn't being treated for it. We're waiting on a toxicology report and hope that will tell us more."

"And the home invaders?" Molly asked.

The officer rolled his eyes. "Have you read the piece in the paper?"

"I haven't had a chance yet," Molly said.

"You probably should," he said. "But remember that nothing from that article originated with the police. Nothing. And that's all I'm going to say about this case. Now, if you'll all excuse me, I need to get to work."

Molly offered an appreciative smile. "Thank you."

"Yeah," Carol called out. "You've been loads of help."

He studied Carol for a moment, clearly suspecting she was being sarcastic. But Carol beamed with the innocence only a grandmother can produce. Molly was impressed.

Molly walked Drummond out of the kitchen. As the officer passed into the customer area, a few people started in his direction, but one glower from him sent them away without a word. When the front door closed behind him, Molly returned to the kitchen.

"We need to know what's in that article," Molly said to Carol and Laura.

"I'll admit, I'm curious," Laura said. "Maybe you could slip out and grab one from the newspaper bin out front?"

Molly felt a bit like a spy as she crept around the building to take a newspaper before anyone could spot her and pelt her with questions. She hurried back inside, shivering. *Next time I play spy, I'm dressing warmer.*

Waving the paper in the air, she headed into the kitchen. "Found it. Do you want me to read it aloud?"

"Sure," Laura said with a grin. "I enjoy story time."

"It'll be interesting to hear the paper read aloud without snorts and sarcasm," Carol added. "Often when Harvey reads me something, it's in the form of a debate with the newspaper."

As Laura chuckled, Molly quickly found the story and began reading. The article reported on Edgar Richardson's work as a police detective, though they made Detroit sound like some sort of cesspool of crime and drugs.

"It's nowhere near that bad," Laura said. "They have wonderful art museums and some amazing restaurants."

"Edgar Richardson must have done an interview with the paper," Molly said. "Probably something for the business section. All the quotes from him seem to be about the bookstore. He said the only crimes he was still interested in were the ones in books."

Carol sighed. "I wish that was the only kind he'd encountered. The poor man comes all the way to Loch Mallaig for a quiet retirement, only to be robbed and die. Does it mention anything about that?"

Molly skipped ahead and read aloud, "A witness who was passing the bookstore on the night of Edgar Richardson's death reports two women hurrying from the scene with their arms full. The police will not comment on these mysterious women, but it leaves us to wonder if a team of female burglars are operating in Loch Mallaig. Books & Bargains may have been their first victim, but who will be their next?" Molly looked up from the paper wide-eyed. "He's talking about Carol and me."

Carol laughed. "We're the violent home invaders?"

"Apparently," Molly said as she scanned the article again. "Why would a reporter say that? Surely even the most cursory follow-up would reveal the women he saw were just us."

"Actually it would be better if the paper never finds that out," Laura said drily. "I'm not sure the *Crown Press* would retract. They'd double down on their theory and name you two as the culprits."

"No one would believe that," Molly insisted, but she had trouble putting much faith behind it. Her experience with some of the gossips of Loch Mallaig was that they'd believe—and spread—almost anything if it was interesting enough.

Carol shook her head. "Harvey is going to tease me into next week."

"This gossip could cast a bad light on the bakehouse," Molly said. "This murder needs to be solved quickly. Maybe I can poke around a little and speed things up."

Laura frowned at her. "I do not think that's a good idea. It could put you in danger."

"It has in the past," Carol added.

Molly couldn't argue with the logic in that, but her mind was made up. She wouldn't have Bread on Arrival tied to that poor man's murder—no matter what.

On most days at Bread on Arrival, the morning rush eventually trailed down, picking up again at lunchtime before slowing to a trickle in the afternoon. That wasn't the case today, however, when it seemed the entire population of Loch Mallaig popped in at some point for a cookie and some gossip. Laura and Carol stayed busy restocking the displays, and Molly even pitched in and mixed up a few batches of shortbread under Carol's watchful eye. Carol insisted Molly didn't need the supervision, but Molly appreciated the support.

It was nearly closing time when Molly slipped through the doorway to the front to see if they were going to need to push people out so they could close. A short line stood at the front counter, their nervous energy suggesting they were waiting for their chance to pepper Bridget with questions. Only Hamish's dour expression kept things moving. Then the line spotted Molly.

"Molly Ferris!" an older man half-shouted. "How did you escape from the burglars during the murder?"

Molly's mouth fell open in surprise at the mishmash of wrong assumptions in the question. "I wasn't around for any murders," she said. "Or burglars."

"That's not what I heard," the man said.

"We know the police are suppressing the real story," the next person in line added.

Hamish clapped his hands. "That's enough. If you're not here for baked goods, then please leave the line."

The first man tried glaring at Hamish for a moment, but soon gave it up. No one was likely to win a glaring contest with Hamish Bruce. "Well, if that's how this shop feels, I'll be going." He left the line and stomped out of the bakery.

"Molly Ferris?" Molly turned to see a pretty, young woman in a stylish wool coat and a knit hat standing well away from the line. Molly was struck immediately by the intense sadness in the newcomer's eyes. "Could I speak to you?"

Molly raised her hands. "I didn't see any murder. Nor any burglary. I simply shopped."

The young woman brightened a little. "That's what I heard from the police. You met my uncle, Edgar Richardson?"

"Your uncle?" Molly repeated in surprise. She immediately realized that their quiet conversation was still too loud in the bakehouse's curiosity-rich atmosphere. The gossips in line had zeroed in on the two of them with fascinated expressions. Molly quickly gestured to the young woman. "Come with me. We'll chat."

Molly led the woman into the back hallway, noting the disappointed murmurs behind them. Since it was so close to closing, Carol and Laura were mostly cleaning up and planning for the following day. They both eyed the young woman curiously as Molly led her into the kitchen.

"Laura Donovan, Carol MacCallan," Molly said, gesturing to each one, "this is Edgar Richardson's niece."

"My name is Chelsea Lowell," she said. "I'm from Normal."

"Normal?" Carol echoed.

"It's a town in Illinois."

Laura's tone was gentle. "We're so sorry for your loss. I didn't get to meet your uncle, but Molly and Carol had only good things to say about him."

"I didn't really know him," Chelsea said. "He and my father had some kind of huge fight years ago, and Uncle Edgar never came to see us after that. I was young and all I remember about him was his height, but I suppose everyone was a giant to me then."

"How can we help you?" Molly asked. "We met your uncle, but any gossip you may have heard about our involvement beyond that was completely fanciful."

"There are many vivid imaginations in Loch Mallaig," Carol added.

Laura pulled off her apron. "Let's have this chat sitting down." She waved toward the chairs near the table where they packed orders for shipping. "Can I get you some coffee?"

"No thanks. I already had quite a bit to keep me alert for the drive," Chelsea said as she followed Laura to the table. She sank into the chair. "As for how you can help, I don't quite know."

"We'll do whatever we can," Molly said as she and the others slipped into the other seats.

"Thank you. I'm not sure what to say, but I suppose I should begin at the beginning. As I said, my father and my uncle had a falling out. For years, Dad wouldn't even allow anyone to mention Uncle Edgar's name to him. Then last year, my father entered a care home. My mom died before the rift between my father and uncle, and I'm an only child, so I had to go through all of Dad's stuff to sort out the finances and such." She sighed deeply. "You know what I mean."

"We do," Molly said.

"Well, I found a bundle of cards from Uncle Edgar to me. Birthday cards mostly, but also two graduation cards, one from high school and one from college. I realized this uncle I never knew had tried to keep a family connection going. I wrote to him then, and we'd been corresponding ever since. We talked about my coming here to visit him, but I wasn't ready for that yet." Chelsea's eyes filled. "I thought I would be soon."

"Take your time," Laura murmured while Carol handed her a box of tissues.

Chelsea nodded and sat quietly for a moment, clearly composing herself. "The police contacted me as next of kin. My father isn't in any condition to speak to them."

Molly felt a stab of sympathy. She doubted this young woman was even as old as her own daughter, and she'd already been through so much.

Chelsea sniffed softly. "Apparently Uncle Edgar also made me his heir, and it seems to be a reasonably large inheritance. I think I'm simply wishing I knew him better. I don't feel like I deserve to inherit anything." Her gaze took in both Carol and Molly. "You both saw him recently. Could you tell me your impressions of him? I'd love to get a sense of him beyond the cards and the e-mails we exchanged."

"He was friendly," Molly said. "And kind, but with a teasing sense of humor, I think. His eyes twinkled when he was thinking of something funny."

"He loved books," Carol offered. "You could tell that right away."

Chelsea perked up a bit. "So do I. We share that."

"Chelsea," Molly said. "Do you have any idea what the fight had been about?"

"It was about my aunt," she answered. "Apparently Dad never approved of his big sister marrying a police officer. He thought it was too dangerous. And then Aunt Annie died and Dad blamed Edgar."

"He thought your uncle killed his wife?" Molly asked, aghast.

Chelsea shook her head so vehemently that her hat slipped. "No, Aunt Annie died in a car accident. But the other vehicle apparently ran Aunt Annie off the road and the driver left her there. The police never found the culprit, and Dad thought they would have if Uncle Edgar had pushed. He thought Uncle Edgar didn't care." Chelsea sighed deeply.

"Uncle Edgar wrote to me about it. He said it's not uncommon for people to blame the police. All their grief has to go somewhere. He didn't seem to blame my dad for it, but I think he was sad."

Molly traded glances with Carol. If Chelsea's dad wasn't in a care home, he would be a good suspect in the murder. "You said your father wasn't in any condition to speak to the police."

"He has Alzheimer's," Chelsea explained. "He has some good days, but he also has some bad ones where he sneaks away from the facility. It's terrifying when he goes missing. Fortunately he's always been found."

"The police said your uncle died of a heart attack," Molly said. "Did he have a heart condition?"

"Maybe." The woman shrugged. "If he did, it isn't something he mentioned to me."

"What did you know about your uncle?" Carol asked.

"I knew he was opening the bookshop." Chelsea gave a wan smile. "He was excited about it. I know he didn't remarry after Aunt Annie. He said he never even came close. He threw himself into his job and only came up for air when he retired." Her gaze grew distant, as if she were reliving the past. "My father described Uncle Edgar as the most self-contained man who ever lived. Dad didn't think that was a virtue."

"It certainly can be," Laura said, earning a side-eye glance from Molly, who wondered at the slightly defensive response. Laura was probably the most self-contained of the three of them.

Chelsea shrugged. "Uncle Edgar was able to save much of his pay over the years, which is how he could retire to Loch Mallaig and buy the bookstore. He sent me pictures of it. I think he was trying to lure me for a visit. I promised to come soon." Her voice sounded choked, and her lower lip trembled.

"You couldn't have predicted what was going to happen," Carol told her.

"I know," Chelsea whispered. "And now I have no family left at all. My mother died years ago of cancer. Dad doesn't know me half the time. And the uncle I was starting to build a relationship with is gone." She looked plaintively from one of them to the next. "Do you think the police will find the people who broke in and brought on the heart attack? It seems to me that someone should be held responsible."

"The Loch Mallaig police are good," Carol said. "And determined. I believe they'll find the truth."

As the young woman nodded, her eyes still full of tears, Molly felt more resolved than ever that she needed to do whatever she could to help. Chelsea needed answers. Molly would make sure she got them.

The opportunity presented itself within the hour when Officer Anderson rapped on the door of the bakehouse shortly after they'd hung the *Closed* sign. "Sorry to keep you," she told Molly when she opened the door. "I was hoping you and Carol could come with me to the bookstore."

"I'm afraid Carol already left," Molly said. "Harvey picked her up, and I think they were going somewhere out of town." Greer groaned, and Molly felt a pang of sympathy. "Want to come in?"

The officer shook her head. "I'll have to try to get a hold of Carol. I would prefer not to do the bookstore walk-through twice. How about tomorrow morning?"

"Two days before Valentine's Day?" Molly said dubiously. "They might be able to spare me, but Carol will be wrist deep in cookie dough all morning. That being said, I'm sure she'll make time to help with such an important investigation. Laura might be a little stressed, but she'll understand. Whatever time Carol agrees to when you speak to her, I'll be available."

"Thanks." A cold rush of air whistled through the open door and both women shivered. "I'll leave you to finish closing up," Greer said. "See you in the morning."

Molly closed out the chilly wind gratefully. She was interested in seeing the bookstore again and hoped they'd notice something to help further the investigation. She suspected that the police wanting Carol and her to revisit the scene of the crime was probably not a good sign. They likely lacked suspects. With a shiver, Molly realized that meant there were still criminals loose in Loch Mallaig.

As it turned out, Laura insisted Molly and Carol go and help the police however they could the next morning. "After hearing that poor girl yesterday," she said, "I think we should do whatever we can. She deserves answers." She waved off their protests about leaving her to manage the bakehouse alone, at least in the kitchen. "I was the head chef in a busy New York restaurant. I think I can manage things here until the police are done with you. Bridget and Hamish will handle the front."

"If you're sure," Carol said. "We won't take longer than we must."

"No," Laura corrected. "You won't take longer than it takes. You're helping the police solve a crime. Go."

They took Molly's little silver Honda Fit for the drive to Books & Bargains. Officer Anderson was already there. As they pulled into the parking lot, she switched off her patrol car with clear reluctance and climbed out, hunching her shoulders against the winter weather.

"Thank you both for coming out," Greer said as she clapped her gloved hands together. "I promise not to keep you longer than necessary."

"We'll do whatever we can," Carol answered as she climbed out of the car. "But I'm not sure what we'll be good for."

"I want to know how the place is different from when you were here," Greer explained.

"We'll do our best," Molly promised.

As soon as they walked into the old farmhouse, Molly immediately spotted change. Shards of ceramic littered the floor. She carefully surveyed the room. "I think that was a vase on this table."

"Anything special about it?" Greer asked.

"I don't think so," Molly said at the same time that Carol offered her opinion that the vase was tacky.

"Do you think this was smashed in anger?" Carol asked. "Or because the burglar was searching for something?"

"We aren't sure. For all we know, it was knocked over by accident." Greer gestured. "Come on through. The biggest mess is at the cash register."

As soon as they stepped into the room, Molly and Carol stopped short with a sharp gasp. The floor was littered with scraps of cardboard, ripped newspaper, books, and broken pottery. Molly realized someone had torn open the boxes from the estate sale and strewn the contents across the weathered hardwood. She didn't see a single curio that was still intact. Fortunately, the books showed much less damage. They simply seemed to have been dumped and perhaps stepped on.

Carol whistled glumly as she slowly surveyed the mess. "Someone was seriously angry."

"Either that, or the person was searching for something." Then Molly shook her head. That theory didn't make sense. Why break small curios? If the thing the person was looking for was that tiny, surely it could fit inside a book. "None of the books appear damaged." Most of the room's shelves were still full of books.

Carol bent and picked up a rumpled paperback. "I don't know about that."

Molly shrugged. "Not intentionally damaged, at least."

"Do either of you know the source of the objects on the floor?" Greer asked. "Did he mention the boxes at all?"

"He did," Molly said. "He'd bought the whole lot from an estate sale. Apparently they were only supposed to contain books, but there were some knickknacks as well." She pointed at a disembodied head laying near her feet. "That was part of a hula dancer. I saw it when he took it out of the box."

"An estate sale?" Greer repeated. "That would give us a place to investigate, though probably not the most promising lead. I'm still leaning toward the robbery angle." She waded through the mess to the counter and tapped a metal box. "This was empty. The vintage cash register is decor as much as anything, I believe."

"He handled the credit card sale with his phone, then printed a receipt for me." Molly peered under the counter. "He had a small printer, but I don't see it."

"We'll put it on the list of stolen items," Greer said. "You didn't see the make of the printer?"

Molly shook her head. "I only noticed it at all because it was small and wireless. I remember thinking it could be useful to have something like that for event booths or other times we're selling outside the bakehouse. I figured I'd ask him about it during some other visit." That thought made her sad again.

"We had hoped to check his receipts to get a picture of his sales in the last few days," Greer said. "The robber may have been in to case the place, but he must keep the receipts somewhere else. Maybe stored in that printer's memory or on his phone."

"Do you have his phone?" Molly asked.

"It was missing."

Molly stared at the metal box absently as she walked her memory back to paying for the dog statue. "He printed two copies of the receipt. I remember clearly. I signed one and he put it in that metal box. I remember it because he asked me to add my e-mail address if I wanted to be on his mailing list."

"That's right," Carol said. "I remember doing that too."

Greer sighed. "Then the culprit must have grabbed the receipts along with the money from the box. All that remained in the box were some business cards."

"Do you have them?" Molly asked.

"At the station, but I do have a list of the businesses." Greer flipped through her notebook and read off a handful of companies.

Molly recognized nearly all the businesses as vendors they'd either used or considered when renovating the bakehouse. Only one was totally new—Morningstar Estate Liquidation. "That's odd," Molly remarked.

"Why's that?" Greer asked. "Didn't you say all this mess came from an estate sale?"

"Well, yes," Molly agreed. "But I remember Ed saying that the estate sale was connected to Lochside Realty somehow." She frowned as she tried to remember. "I'm not sure of his exact words, but I know he mentioned Lochside."

Greer shrugged. "Maybe the two companies are connected somehow. I'll check it out." The officer jotted a note, but something in her tone suggested she didn't consider it important.

Standing near the counter, Molly surveyed the room one more time. Was there some pattern to the mess? She couldn't tell, other than it clearly all came from the boxes Ed had been unpacking. She nudged a book with her toe and wondered how long it would take to clean up the mess. She supposed it would be Chelsea Lowell's job eventually. Molly made a mental note to offer to help.

"You ladies are free to go," Greer said after she finished making notes. "I appreciate you both coming over here. There was always the possibility that being here would jog an important memory."

"It's jogged some sad ones," Carol said.

Molly's gaze remained on the discarded books around the register. Why destroy the crockery but not the books? If the burglar was enraged, she supposed the breaking of china was more satisfying than stomping a few paperbacks. She spotted a piece of ceramic in the shape of a ukulele and knew it too came from the campy hula dancer. She bent to pick it up—and saw a piece of folded paper obscured by the shadow of the counter. "What's this?"

She had already scooped it up when Greer warned, "Don't touch it."

Molly grimaced sheepishly. "Sorry about that. Fingerprints, right?"

"It's probably nothing," Greer said, "but put it here on the counter and we'll unfold it with gloved hands."

Molly dropped the folded paper on the counter.

Once Greer had donned latex gloves, she opened the note. All three women stared at the simple block letters.

I'LL NEVER FORGET WHAT YOU DID!

7

Molly took an involuntary step away from the note. Beside her, Carol said, "That certainly sounds ominous."

"Possibly." Greer slipped the note into an evidence bag. "It sounds bad in light of the murder, but we don't know the context. It could easily have been a note of thanks for something the man did in the line of duty. I'm sure there are people who will never forget things Mr. Richardson did when he was a detective."

"And some of them were probably angry," Carol pointed out. "Are you checking into people he put in prison who are now out?"

"We are," Greer said shortly, clearly less than pleased to have the police's methods questioned.

"I'm sure you'll sort it out," Molly said soothingly. She wasn't interested in seeing her friends snipe at one another. She also didn't believe for an instant that the paper she'd found was a note of gratitude. She'd certainly never sent a thank-you note without signing it, or even including the words "thank you." And stark block letters were traditionally how people tried to hide their handwriting, weren't they?

"Again, thank you both for coming out and revisiting the scene," Greer said. "But I know you need to get to work."

"We do," Molly said. "If you find out the context for the note, would you let me know?"

Greer raised an eyebrow. "You know I can't comment on open cases."

Since she'd done exactly that many times before, both Molly and Carol gazed at her silently until Greer squirmed a little. "If it's something I can share, I'll call you."

"Thank you," Molly said, then she picked her way through the mess on the floor and headed toward the door with Carol right behind her. Greer followed so closely in their wake that Molly felt hustled out the door.

As they drove to Bread on Arrival, Molly mentally ran through the few bits they'd learned. She assumed Carol was doing the same since they rode in relative silence. Molly felt sure the note was every bit as ominous as it sounded, but she had no related leads to pursue. She did know the name of the estate sale company, though, and since the bulk of the destruction seemed focused on the estate sale boxes, Molly decided to focus her efforts in that direction.

"Have you ever heard of Morningstar Estate Liquidation?" Molly asked Carol.

"No," Carol said. "Maybe it's new."

"Maybe, or maybe we haven't heard of it because neither of us has needed that particular service. But it's the only thing I can think of to pursue. If you and Laura can spare me for a few more minutes when we get back, I'm going up to the office to search for the company online."

Carol cut her eyes toward Molly. "You could use your phone."

Molly groaned. "I do not enjoy trying to read web pages on my phone. It reminds me that I have the vision of someone over fifty."

Carol hooted. "Tell me about it. And Harvey is even worse. He refuses to put on his reading glasses half the time and just holds the newspaper at arm's length to read it. He always looks like he's trying to play the trombone."

Molly pulled her Honda into a parking space, and Carol immediately opened her door. "You should go up the outside stairs to the apartment and avoid the lure of work," Carol suggested. "Come down when you have information to share."

Molly chuckled, cheered to know Carol was as curious as she was. She locked up her car and headed for the fenced area at the base of the stairs. The area served as Angus's romping space during work hours, though Molly wasn't above slipping out now and then to give the little Scottie a walk. Angus was a good dog, but he needed new experiences to keep him from letting boredom lead him into trouble.

As she reached the fence, Angus dashed over from the other side of the stairs and yipped happily, his whole body wiggling with joy. "I'm glad to see you too," Molly said as she let herself into the yard and scooped him up. The way he bathed her chin in doggy kisses, Molly was tempted to check her watch to see if she'd left him behind much longer than she thought. "It's nice to be missed," she told him.

She set him down, and he bounded up the stairs and into the bakery office beside her. Most of the upper floor of the bakehouse was taken up by Molly's cozy apartment, with the bakery office being the only business area. Molly was in the office most since she handled the bakery's promotions and the online sales, though Carol, a retired math teacher, used it as well to handle the bookkeeping.

Angus danced around Molly's feet until she settled into the office chair. At that point, he offered one last yip before flopping onto a cushion in the corner and eyeing her sulkily. "We'll do something fun soon," she promised him. In response, he merely rearranged himself on the cushion so that she could only see his back.

Chuckling at her dog's dramatics, Molly powered on the computer. While it booted up, she walked through Books & Bargains in her head. The shop hadn't been exactly orderly when Molly had first visited with Carol, but the disarray she'd seen this morning was extreme. It felt violent and angry in a way that seemed personal. That brought her thoughts to Ed's neighbor. Myron Webster came across as angrier than someone who simply didn't want a shop in his neighborhood.

Of course Molly knew people could be defensive about their homes. *Maybe I'm reading too much into it.* She was glad when the computer was ready and she could focus her attention on finding new information instead of letting her thoughts swirl in circles.

She typed *Morningstar Estate Liquidation* into the search engine and was surprised to see the company was located in Ann Arbor. Was that where the estate had been?

She poked around the website, hoping for a list of recent sales. Perhaps she could guess at the source of the boxes. She didn't find such a list, but she did come across an announcement that the company was expanding with several small satellite branches—and one of them was in Loch Mallaig. Molly clicked on a link and then stared in surprise at a familiar face. Beverly Scott, attractive and stylish as always, smiled out at her.

"So you're doing estate sales on the side?" Molly asked the photo aloud. Molly was on friendly terms with the woman who had sold them the bakehouse, but Carol and Laura knew Beverly better since they attended Fair Knitting Ladies meetings together. "Clearly my next source is downstairs—along with some work, no doubt."

If Angus had a response to his person talking to herself, he didn't bother to share it. Molly left him snoozing on the cushion when she headed down to the bakehouse.

"Molly," Laura called as soon as she walked into the kitchen. "Can you jump on the mail orders? It's been ridiculously busy this morning, and neither Hamish nor Bridget has had a spare minute to pack them up."

"Of course." Molly saw Laura had rolled a rack of pastries and cookies over to the packing table, and she quickly began going through the list of orders to see what she needed to fill. In minutes, she had things sorted and began folding up her first shipping box.

Carol walked over to the table and slid a tray of cookies into the rack. "Don't pack these right away. The icing needs to set. Did you find anything about the estate sale company?"

"I did," Molly replied as she carefully folded tissue into the shipping box. "They are out of Ann Arbor, but they've opened some satellite branches. One is here in Loch Mallaig, and Beverly Scott is running it."

"Beverly?"

"Her photo was on the website." Molly carefully counted cookies into a paper tray, then began wrapping the tray of cookies with shrink wrap. "I take it she didn't mention it."

"No, though our conversations are generally more about knitting and family," Carol said. "The Fair Knitting Ladies is an escape from work."

"I can understand that. I wonder if she handled the estate sale where Ed Richardson bought all those boxes of books and curios," Molly said. "If she did, maybe she could tell us where they originated."

"You think that's relevant?"

"I think we're always better off to know something than to not know it." Molly picked up the heat gun they used to seal the shrink wrap and plugged it in.

"I'll call her when we get a break," Carol said. "For now, I'd better ice more cookies before Laura strains her eyes glaring at us."

Molly peeked at their friend across the room and caught a steely glint in her eyes. "Yes, we should definitely put the sleuthing on the back burner for a while."

"Agreed."

Carol hurried away, and Molly gave her full attention to the order list. With a sigh, she eyed the pretty little heart cookies she'd finished sealing. They were darling, and she appreciated the boost in business from the holiday, but Valentine's Day wasn't very exciting for single people who weren't dating.

Not that I mind not dating. I'm an independent woman with plenty of things to do. But as she thought about the past giddy joys of having a little romance in her life—her late husband, Kevin, had been wonderfully thoughtful—Molly had to admit, she missed it.

The rest of the day passed almost too quickly as the rush never let up. It seemed everyone in Loch Mallaig wanted something from Bread on Arrival. In fact, Molly was heading for the front for an energy-boosting cup of coffee when she heard Hamish gently shooing people out at closing time. Well, gentle for Hamish anyway.

"Go on home with you," he ordered, his rough voice brooking no argument.

Molly glanced over at Laura, who was wiping counters. Laura sometimes scolded Hamish for being gruff with patrons, but as far as Molly could tell, everyone loved Hamish no matter how grumbly he became. And since he'd managed the front alone for the last hour after Bridget left to catch one of her college lectures, Molly felt he deserved some leeway.

I didn't realize it was so late. Molly decided to hold off on the coffee until after she finished up the last orders for shipping. She returned to the shipping table, affixed labels to the last boxes, and added them to the pile. Hamish walked into the room as Molly was checking off the final item on the list.

"I can drop those boxes off," he offered as he wrapped a scarf around his neck.

"Thanks," Molly replied. "I figured I'd take them, but I should probably walk Angus. Last I saw him, he was unhappy with me."

Hamish smiled, though the quirk of his lips was quickly replaced with his usual stern expression. "I'm sure Angus has gotten over himself by now. You don't want to coddle the lad too much."

"I'll keep that in mind," Molly assured him with a grin.

"I'm going by Lochside Realty on my way home," Carol said. "I never had a chance to call Beverly, but she should still be in the office."

"Unless she's out showing a house," Laura volunteered as she slipped out of her apron. "Not that I imagine they sell many homes this time of year."

"Give me a call if she says anything interesting," Molly said to Carol.

"Sure, though probably not before dinner. Harvey's got a poker game tonight so we're eating early." Carol buttoned her coat up to her neck and waved to all of them before heading for the door.

Laura paused on her own way out. "It's always amazing to me how quiet the bakery gets after closing."

"You should try living above it," Molly remarked.

Laura withdrew a knit hat from her coat pocket and pulled it on. "No thanks. I'll take my little cottage. I'm like Goldilocks—I've found something just right for me."

"I think we all have." Molly walked Laura and Hamish to the back door, then locked up. She took one last tour of the downstairs, not expecting to find anything out of place but simply to be certain. As Laura had pointed out, the room was startlingly quiet. Hamish had put out the fire in the fireplace, though the room was still wonderfully toasty. Molly touched one of the fireplace stones, enjoying the warmth seeping into her hand.

"Oh well, time to go out in the cold." She returned to the back hallway and went up the stairs, calling as she climbed. "Angus? You ready for a walk?"

The excited barking from the other side of the apartment door was all the answer she needed.

After a long stroll through Dumfries Park with Angus, Molly was happy to get home to her warm, snug apartment. She and Angus spent a quiet evening together curled up on the sofa as Molly finished the novel she'd gotten from Books & Bargains. Ed had been right—it was wonderful. She felt a pang at the fact that she wouldn't be able to tell him how much she'd enjoyed it.

That sadness followed her to bed, and it took entirely too long to slip into a troubled sleep. She dreamed that she was searching for someone in a maze of twelve-foot-tall bookshelves.

Her bedroom was pitch-dark when Molly was awakened by a frantically barking Angus. She nearly fell out of bed in her hurry to reach him and found the little Scottie standing at the door to the interior stairs, pawing at the threshold as he sounded the alarm.

Molly raced into the kitchen and snatched up her phone from where she'd left it charging. If she was going downstairs to confront who-knew-what in the bakehouse, she would do it with her phone in hand. When she reached the apartment door, Molly bent and scooped up her dog, tucking him under one arm. "You'd best come with me," she said. "I don't want to trip over you on the stairs."

Angus didn't even glance at her. His attention was totally focused on the apartment door. Molly hesitated and put her ear to the wood. Since Angus wouldn't stop barking and growling, she couldn't hear anything else. "I hope you scared it away," she whispered. "Whatever it was."

She opened the door and flipped on the stairway light. It did little to disturb the shadows at the bottom, but at least it allowed her to get down the steps safely. As if realizing Molly needed to focus, Angus fell silent in her arms. She paused at the bottom landing, and her heart seemed to leap into her throat as she heard the clear sound of someone moving around in the kitchen.

Angus must have heard the person as well. He burst into a flurry of barking and growling. "I can hear you!" Molly shouted toward the kitchen. "And I've already called the police!"

The words were barely out of her mouth before she saw movement at the kitchen doorway. Molly jumped away in alarm. As she did, she heard something whiz straight toward her in the dark and strike the wall beside her head with an ominously loud *whack.*

8

With her heart pounding in her throat, Molly crouched with her arms around Angus. The dog must have been surprised by Molly's sudden movements because he'd stopped barking. From her position near the floor, Molly caught a glimpse of a slim figure in a hooded sweatshirt sprinting toward the rear entrance. She heard the door bang open. For a long moment, she simply could not move, as if all her joints had been locked by fear.

Without changing position, she managed to call the police on her cell—the call she'd bluffed about when addressing the intruder. As soon as she finished, Angus lapped her chin. "Sorry," she whispered to him. "I'm not as brave as you."

With no further sound coming from the back door or anywhere else in the bakery, Molly finally unfolded from her crouch and crept down the hall to the rear entrance. She pulled the sleeve of her robe over her hand so she wouldn't leave prints on top of the intruder's, then closed the door and locked it.

Once the door was secure, Molly backtracked through the bakehouse, flipping on every possible light. Soon the kitchen was as bright as day, and Angus set to work patrolling the baseboards.

Molly wrapped her arms around herself and finally did the one thing she'd been avoiding. She took a steadying breath and eyed the spot on the wall where she'd heard something strike. With horror, she saw Laura's best chef's knife embedded in the wall, its blade gleaming wickedly. That was when the shaking started, and Molly had to sit down before her knees could buckle.

The sound of the bakery's front door opening snapped Molly from her daze. Angus raced for the café area before Molly could catch him. How was someone coming in the front door? She couldn't leave Angus to face someone alone, so she ran after him.

"Mrs. Ferris?" a male voice called from the front as Molly burst through the doorway. Officer Michael Drummond stood near the open door, bending slightly to examine the lock.

"I'm right here. How did you get in?" she asked, her voice sounding unnaturally high even to her own ears.

"The door was open," he said. "Someone picked the lock. Not well, but apparently well enough."

Angus had crossed the room to sniff at the officer. Molly grabbed him so he wouldn't interfere. "The intruder left through the back."

"Then I'll check out in the yard too," he said. "Stay right here."

"I won't move an inch," Molly assured him.

Drummond nodded and closed the front door, then walked through the bakehouse to the rear entrance. Molly tried to focus on how the glow of the porch light faintly illuminated the bread loaves and Celtic knots depicted in the custom stained glass window. She was straining to suppress an urge to scour the entire bakehouse to rid it of any trace of a knife-wielding burglar. Fortunately the officer's search didn't take long.

"The ground is too hard for tracks," he said when he returned. "I saw the knife in the wall near the stairs. Go ahead and tell me what happened."

Molly recounted her experience, starting with being awakened by Angus. Her voice got a little shaky as she described the knife whizzing by her head, but otherwise she was proud of her clear recitation. She finished with hearing the back door close. "I called the police after that. I didn't go outside to see if I could catch sight of the intruder."

Drummond's expression was shocked. "I should hope not. The person had already showed a willingness to hurt you. You could have been seriously injured—or worse. The next time Angus alerts you to something going on downstairs, stay upstairs and call 911."

The next time? Molly swallowed down a lump of fear. She had no interest in arguing the wisdom of what she'd done. She was all too aware. "You're right."

"Okay, let me take some photos and dust for prints," the officer said. "And you should call a locksmith and change your front door lock to one that's a bit harder to pick. I'm not inclined to leave you here alone when the front door is compromised."

Molly glanced at the time. "Actually, Laura and Carol will probably be here before you're done. We start early in a bakery."

"Good. In the meanwhile, you should probably sit down. You're still a good bit paler than usual. I don't want you fainting on me."

Again Molly was shaky enough that she felt no urge to argue. She settled in one of the rough-hewn chairs and held Angus in her lap while the officer carefully went through the bakehouse. Since she wasn't needed, she made calls to Carol and Laura, hoping she wasn't catching either of them in bed. She wasn't, and they both promised to be in as quickly as possible. Her friends spoke with such concern for her that Molly had to fight tears more than once before she got off the phone.

Finally Officer Drummond called her into the kitchen. "You said the intruder was in here when you came down. Could you take a look around and tell me if anything appears to be missing?"

As Laura and Carol were both fastidious about the placement of everything in the kitchen, it was easy to see that little had even been disturbed, much less gone missing. Only the knife projecting from the wall showed obvious signs of the intruder's passing.

"Do you keep money or valuables down here anywhere?" the officer asked.

Molly shrugged. "That knife in the wall is worth more than whatever we'd have in the till, but I can check the register." She did and saw nothing had been tampered with out front either. The only surprise came when she noticed a change in the decorations in front of the fireplace and on the mantel. Nothing was missing, but everything appeared to have been shifted around slightly. She frowned and reported that to Drummond, who had followed her to the café. "Why would anyone mess with this stuff?" she asked. "None of it's valuable."

"It does make me wonder if the intruder was searching for something. Perhaps he or she got the impression some of this was antique," the officer suggested.

"Maybe," Molly said. "The display counters are. I suppose that might make someone think we decorate with antiques." It didn't seem likely, but she had no other explanation.

Carol arrived as the officer was finishing up and immediately gave Molly a warm hug. "I'm here now. Do you need to go up and change?"

Molly glanced down at her robe. She'd forgotten that she was still in her pajamas. "I should. Will you be okay? The front door lock was picked and Officer Drummond says we should get a new lock."

Carol tutted. "I'll be perfectly safe. Picking locks is more the work of a sneak. He's not likely to mess with an angry woman with a rolling pin in her hands, and Laura should be here any minute. And don't rush. You've been through enough for the morning."

"Well, I probably should walk Angus," Molly said. "If you're sure."

Carol flapped her hands. "Go! I want to check the door. I hope Hamish knows someone who can change the lock today. I'm fairly sure Loch and Key is closed. The owner only opens a couple times a week in January and February. He's an ice-fishing fanatic, according to Harvey."

"I'm sure Hamish can replace the lock himself," Molly said. Technically Hamish was their handyman, though he spent more time working the counter than fixing leaky sinks and creaky hinges. "And I imagine he'd be insulted if we suggested otherwise."

"I expect you're right." Carol shooed her away again, and Molly took the hint. She headed upstairs, grateful for her friend, who had already made her feel considerably better.

By the time Molly had dressed, eaten breakfast, and walked Angus, Bread on Arrival was open for the day. When she walked down the sidewalk with Angus in tow, she spotted Hamish stooped over the front door knob and felt a bit of tension ease. At least the door would soon be fixed.

She walked Angus around and headed up the exterior stairs to the apartment. As she prepared to leave him for the day, she gave him an extra treat. "I'm not making a habit of this," she warned him. "But you did a great job last night."

Angus carried his reward to the closest dog bed and flopped down to enjoy it as Molly headed for the office to grab any orders that had come in overnight. Unsurprisingly with Valentine's Day so close, the number had fallen off sharply. "I guess the window for shipping Valentine's treats has closed," she said to herself as she gathered up orders and headed downstairs.

As soon as she entered the kitchen, Carol and Laura demanded to know if she was okay before letting her get to work. "That must have been terrifying," Laura said.

"Well," Molly said, trying for a light tone, "the knife-throwing was exciting."

Laura shuddered at that and gestured toward her knife rack with the dough scraper in her hand. "Maybe we should lock those up at night, or at least put them in a drawer out of sight. I could take them home with me too. I never need most of them as a baker except to chop nuts and chocolate, and I might get more use out of them at the cottage."

"If you need them at home, go for it, but I'm not sure we should overreact," Molly said. "I wasn't hurt, and I should have called the police from upstairs."

"And stayed there." Laura cut a piece of dough from the huge lump in front of her with a little more force than was necessary. "But what are the odds you'll start doing that?"

Since Molly couldn't imagine hiding upstairs and not knowing what was going on in their beloved bakehouse, she didn't want to continue the conversation. Instead, she waved the printout in her hand. "Can we focus on work, please? I'll fill these few orders for mailing." She headed over to the packing table. "Carol, did Beverly say anything interesting about the estate sale company?"

"I didn't get to talk to her," Carol answered as she carried a cake from the freezer to the decorating table. "The office was closed when I got there. I'll try again today, though."

Molly didn't comment, but as she tackled the orders for shipping, she found herself growing increasingly antsy. She needed to do something about the mystery in front of them, especially since she wasn't sure the break-in at the bakehouse was unrelated. She broached that theory with Laura and Carol.

Laura gaped at her. "You think the same burglar broke in here?"

"I don't know," Molly admitted. "The timing feels too coincidental, though."

"Maybe the local gossip is right," Carol suggested. "Perhaps someone is launching a string of burglaries on Loch Mallaig businesses. We could have been number two."

"If so, the burglar is making fairly unlucrative choices," Laura said as she expertly rolled dough into neat bun shapes. "Used bookstores and bakeries aren't exactly known for their valuables."

"Whoever broke in did mess with the things around the fireplace," Molly said. "Maybe searching for valuables?"

"Among that stuff?" Laura shook her head. "I mean, it's cute decor and I like it, but none of it is expensive. The person would have been better off grabbing kitchen equipment."

"Maybe he would have," Carol said, "if Molly hadn't come down with Angus. We don't know what the plan was since he clearly didn't finish. It's possible the burglar checked out the fireplace first simply because it's closer to the door than the register or the kitchen."

"I suppose, but then the burglaries wouldn't be connected with the estate sale, right?" Laura insisted. "After all, we haven't been to any estate sales lately."

"We don't actually know what any connections there are," Molly said. "Or if any exist. But I think I need to talk to Beverly." She eyed the order table. "Once I finish these, I'm going to drive over. I'm restless today, and I think I'll feel better if I get out of the bakehouse."

"I can't blame you for that," Carol said. "Not after last night."

"And if it'll make you feel better, then you should go," Laura added supportively. "In fact, don't worry about the orders. You can do them when you get back, or we'll put Hamish on it when he's done grumbling at that 'newfangled' lock set he's installing."

Molly reached for her coat, but hesitated. "If you're sure you don't mind."

"Go," Carol and Laura ordered in unison, then chuckled at their chorus.

Molly didn't give them time to change their minds. She slung her coat on and headed out the back door while her friends' laughter still hung in the air. Outside, she saw Angus in the fenced-in yard, radiating hope with every fiber of his small body. "I was hoping to sneak off while you were napping upstairs," she told him. The little dog wagged his tail. "I guess I owe you an outing for being my hero. Come on." She opened the gate and scooped him up before he could dash out. She kept a spare leash in her car.

In warmer weather, Molly and Angus would have walked to Lochside Realty. It wasn't close, but nothing in the business district was terribly far. Today, however, the chill in the air and the random icy spots on the sidewalks made the thought of a long trek far less appealing. The drive to the office was quick, but a big surprise waited at the other end.

A police car was parked outside the real estate office, and the glass in the door was broken near the lock. Was this the work of the same burglar? Molly and Angus joined the crowd gathering on the sidewalk. Clearly the people of Loch Mallaig could tolerate a little cold in order to satisfy their curiosity.

Officer Drummond stepped through the door as Molly reached the crowd. A rotund man in a plaid coat called out, "Is this part of the chain of burglaries?"

The officer held up both hands. "Let's not jump to conclusions."

"Jump to conclusions?" the man shouted back. "The killer burglars have broken into three businesses now. I heard all about how one of the bakers at Bread on Arrival was attacked with a knife and is in the hospital."

"I'm all right actually," Molly said, but the man never even glanced her way.

"No one is in the hospital," Officer Drummond responded firmly.

"Did she die?" Molly's attention flashed to the crowd. Who had asked that horrible question? She couldn't be sure.

A woman near the shouting man added her angry voice to the din.

"How long before the murderers start coming after regular citizens? I'm scared to close my eyes at night now."

"We have no reason to panic," Drummond said.

"Of course you don't," the man snapped. "You carry a weapon."

Officer Drummond recognized Molly in the crowd and beckoned her forward. "This is Molly Ferris," he said. "She scared away the burglar at Bread on Arrival, and you can all see that she is the picture of health. Now, please, everyone go home."

"Fine, but when I get there, I'm putting some new locks on my doors and windows," the woman announced.

But despite more grumbling, seeing Molly did seem to take the wind out of the bystanders' sails and they began to dissipate.

"Did you need to see me?" the officer asked her quietly as he led her into the building.

"No," Molly said honestly. "I had no idea you were here. I came to chat with Beverly Scott."

"Good. She could probably use a friend right now. Especially since I need to be going." He patted Angus and started to head outside.

Molly caught his arm. "Do you think this could be the same person who broke into Bread on Arrival? And if so, why didn't he simply pick the lock again?"

The officer stared at her without speaking for a long moment before giving in. "He tried picking the lock first. I saw the scratches. The locks here are more expensive than yours. I imagine he gave up on it and went with a more dramatic entrance."

Molly shuddered at the thought of Bread on Arrival's beautiful stained glass window scattered across the floor in pieces. She thanked the officer, and he left.

Molly surveyed the front room of the real estate office. The reception desk was messy, with papers scattered across the surface and more on the floor, but otherwise the room seemed normal enough. "Beverly?" Molly called out.

The stylish woman stepped through the door from the inner office and offered Molly a weak smile. "Molly, how can I help you?"

"Are you okay?" Molly asked.

Beverly began aimlessly straightening papers on the reception desk. "I'm a little freaked out, but I'll be all right. I cannot imagine why someone would want to break into a real estate office. We don't keep money here."

"I spent the morning asking the same thing about the bakehouse." Molly held tight to Angus's leash so he couldn't wander near the door and the scatter of glass. "These break-ins don't make much sense."

"No, not really." Beverly stopped shuffling papers and took a deep breath. "I have to wait around for someone to replace the door glass, so I think I'm going to make some coffee. Want some?"

"Thank you," Molly said and followed Beverly through the doorway into a large office. "Can I ask you something about Books & Bargains? Edgar told me he'd bought some books from an estate sale. Were you connected with that?"

"I was." Beverly waved Molly toward a nearby chair, then walked over to a long counter set up at one end of the room as a coffee station. "We decided to partner with a company out of Ann Arbor so we could add estate sales as an ancillary business to the realty side. Sales can be slow in the winter, so having another source of income is a good idea for a business that relies on commissions. Of course Heath Bruce takes a more hands-off approach to owning Lochside Realty, so I took on most of the duties."

"That must keep you busy," Molly said, impressed that Beverly managed it all with a school-age daughter at home.

"It does, but I don't mind. It's mostly phone calls to coordinate things like the packing up of the items after they're sold."

"So you didn't pack the boxes that went to Edgar Richardson?"

"No, and he called to let me know whoever had packed the boxes included more than books." Beverly made a face. "I probably shouldn't have hired high school kids for that job, but they work cheap."

"What estate was this?"

"Emily Finch," Beverly said as she popped a small pod into the single-cup coffee maker and pushed a button.

Molly scrolled through her mental files. "The name doesn't sound familiar."

"She was a delightful person, a retired schoolteacher from Ohio. I only knew her because she'd been a member of the Fair Ladies Knitting group some years back. She had to quit when she got so sick. I used to drop by and visit. She loved company. Cream or sugar?"

"A little cream, thanks," Molly said. "It was kind of you to keep her company."

Beverly laughed as she doctored the first mug of coffee and started another cup brewing. "It was self-serving. Emily knew more about knitting than I ever will, and she was always willing to share. I sometimes took projects with me that had me baffled. One peek and Emily could tell me what was wrong every time." She carried the prepared mug to Molly. "I liked her."

"So you handled her estate sale," Molly said, taking the hot coffee.

Beverly sank into a nearby chair. "And Lochside will be handling the sale of her cottage for her grandson. He is the one who asked us to handle liquidating the contents as well, though we were to reserve anything of real value so he could examine it. We didn't actually find anything to hold back. A few minor antiques, but nothing particularly valuable. Emily seemed to invest mostly in books and yarn, neither of which had a huge resale value."

"Was the grandson expecting her to have valuables?" Molly asked.

"Apparently so." Beverly retrieved her cup of coffee from the machine. She took a sip and smiled. "I needed that. Anyway, the grandson was disappointed. He said the house should have contained some valuable jewelry, family heirlooms." She lifted a shoulder in shrug. "I suspect Emily may have sold the jewelry. She had a full-time nurse in her last months, and that kind of care is expensive."

"Did you tell the grandson as much?"

"I did. In fact, we have had some heated conversations on the phone and in person. Mr. Mitchum has all but accused us of stealing the jewelry."

"Is he local?"

Beverly shook his head. "He lives in Indianapolis but drove to Loch Mallaig when we didn't find the items he seemed to expect. The sale had already taken place by the time he got here. He complained about that as well, even though he'd told us that he was in a big hurry." She sighed. "Honestly, he's a tiresome person."

"Is he still here?" Molly asked.

"I have no idea." Beverly took another sip of her coffee. "I'll be happy to avoid him. He seems to have given up on calling to berate us, so maybe he's gone home. I'll be perfectly happy not to see his weaselly face again."

Molly grinned and raised an eyebrow at her.

Beverly's expression grew embarrassed. "Listen to me. I'm not usually one to talk about clients, especially like that. My nerves must be worse than I thought. I'm sure he doesn't really resemble a weasel. He's simply a very thin man who could shave a bit more often." She put her hand to her mouth. "See? I'm doing it again. I should probably avoid people for the rest of the day. The stress is making me cranky."

"That's completely forgivable," Molly assured her. "You said Emily Finch had a full-time nurse. Did you meet her?"

"A few times when I visited." Beverly rolled her eyes. "She was another piece of work. Poor Emily. I can't imagine the stress of being terribly sick and having to deal with a cranky grandson and a bossy nurse. It's enough to make me worry about my golden years."

"Do you remember the woman's name?"

Beverly thought about it for a moment. "Her last name was Paterson," she said. "Her first name was Edna—no, Ida. Ida Paterson. Why? Do you think it matters?"

"I don't know if the nurse has any bearing on the burglaries, but the more information I'm armed with, the better."

"I don't know what service she was with," Beverly said. "There are only two in the area, though. Helping Hearts Health Care is probably the most used, and then there's Traveling Care."

Molly thanked her for the information and took her leave. On her way back to the bakehouse, she reflected that Sean Mitchum was probably a better suspect than the nurse. He had already been aggressive about the jewelry he'd expected to find. She thought she ought to find out if he was still in Loch Mallaig.

Was it possible that a bitter man had taken to breaking and entering on a hunt for his grandmother's jewelry?

At the Bread on Arrival parking lot, Molly leaned into her Honda to untangle Angus's leash, which had gotten twisted in a seat belt. Though her hands were occupied with the task at hand, her mind was still trying to sort out all the information she knew. She felt as if she only needed to get the details grouped properly and she'd see the big picture, the one that would reveal the killer.

Thus occupied, Molly didn't hear the footsteps approaching her from behind. And when a deep voice said her name, she shrieked and jolted up so fast that she smacked her head on the hard edge of the car's doorframe.

"Oh, Molly. I snuck up on you again. I'm so sorry."

She turned to see Fergus, the remorse on his face reminding her somehow of the boy she'd known so many years before. Had Fergus looked guilty that often then? Probably so—although always kindhearted, he'd been a mischievous kid who loved finding fun, often in unexpected ways.

Rubbing her head, she offered a forgiving smile. "I'm okay. Can I help you with something?"

"Actually, I came by to check on you," he said. "I heard about the break-in. You should have called me. I'd have been right over."

"I appreciate that. I've had a crazy morning, or I would have called." Molly stopped rubbing her head and reached in to finish untangling Angus. Once free, he bounded out of the car and greeted Fergus, who reached out to pet the little dog. Angus received the petting with his usual delight.

"I can send over some of the security staff from Castleglen for tonight," he offered.

"That's nice of you, but I think we're okay. Castleglen would probably be a more appealing target than Bread on Arrival now. The burglar has to know we don't have much."

"So you think it was a simple burglary?" Fergus asked, his expression doubtful.

"It appears to be part of a series. The bookstore, the bakehouse, and Lochside Realty. I was just over there, and the burglar gained entrance in a similar way, trying to pick the front door lock before giving up and breaking a glass in the door."

"The front door?" Fergus's expression darkened. "That's bold, even in the middle of the night. Both businesses are right on the street. Anyone could have seen the crimes in progress."

"In theory, I suppose," Molly agreed. "Though not many people are out and about in Loch Mallaig at night in February. As soon as the sun goes down, it's brutally cold."

"I suppose."

"Speaking of cold, I'm not all that comfortable standing still out here now. I ought to walk Angus around a little. Do you want to join me?"

Fergus's expression brightened and his blue eyes twinkled. "Happily." They walked toward the street in companionable silence, then he asked, "Are you doing anything for Valentine's Day?"

Molly laughed and answered in a campy Southern belle impression, "I would, but I simply cannot choose between my many suitors."

"Oh, of course, Miss Scarlett," he said, then winced. "Maybe not Miss Scarlett. That makes me think of *Clue*, which is a little too close for comfort."

"A little," Molly agreed. "Are you hosting any special events at Castleglen for Valentine's Day?"

"Not exactly, though we temporarily added fondue and chocolate mousse to the menu at King's Heid Pub," he said.

"Was that your idea or Neil's?" Molly asked. Fergus's son, Neil, assisted him at the resort as he learned the ropes of the family business.

"Neil's," Fergus answered with fatherly pride. "He also talked me into some rearranging of tables at the restaurant in case couples want to dance. That and some heart decor is about as far as we're going."

"I know a thing or two about hearts," Molly replied. "I think I've packed a million heart cookies for mail order sales this month." Then she gave him a crooked smile. "Maybe not a million, but some days it felt like it."

"I've never completely understood Valentine's Day," Fergus said. "I would hope men aren't so desperately in need of the reminder to be romantic. Personally, I enjoy being romantic."

Molly gave him a side-eye glance. "Really? Like how?"

He chuckled. "Can't give up all my secrets. Besides, I know you—you'll laugh at me."

Molly began to protest, but gave it up. "Maybe," she admitted. "But only a little. Romance can be fun, but I prefer it not to feel forced."

"Fair point," Fergus said. "On the other hand, there are some great sales on chocolate right afterward. When I was kid, I'd save up for the chocolate holidays."

"Valentine's Day, Easter, and Halloween?"

"Exactly," he agreed. "Christmas too, but not as much."

While they'd chatted about the holiday, they had taken a short walk to the end of the street and back. Molly felt surprisingly better, as if the weight of her fear and worry had lifted, at least a little. She stopped in the grass at Bread on Arrival. "Thank you for coming by," she said. "I really am feeling better."

"Then I've done my duty." Fergus bowed. "But seriously, call or text me if you change your mind about the security. I'll send them right over if it'll make you feel better."

"That's not necessary," she said. "*You* made me feel better." As if in agreement, Angus gave a single enthusiastic yip, making Molly and Fergus both laugh.

After she brought Angus upstairs, where he settled down for a nap, Molly checked for new orders on the computer, then went to the kitchen. She told Carol and Laura about the break-in at the real estate office.

"Oh, poor Beverly," Carol said. "Was Heath Bruce there?"

"No," Molly said. "But based on something Beverly said, I don't think he's there that often."

"Even if he wasn't there, he must know about the break-in." Carol walked across the room and called through the door, "Hamish, can you spare a minute?"

"Almost," he responded, his voice as gruff as ever.

When he walked into the kitchen, Carol asked, "Lochside Realty was just broken into. Did your nephew mention anything about it to you?"

"Not a word," Hamish said. "Though it's not as if Heath would call me."

"Not even to ask you to fix the door?" Laura chimed in.

"The villain broke a door?" Hamish's snowy eyebrows raised. "Why not pick the lock, same as here?"

"Michael Drummond said the guy tried picking the lock and apparently gave it up for easier access," Molly said. "That's assuming it was a man. I didn't see the person clearly, though I'm fairly sure it was someone taller than me."

Hamish snorted. "I've seen birds taller than you, lass."

Molly took a breath to defend herself, but decided against it.

Knowing Hamish's love of birds, he could potentially name a half dozen that actually were taller than Molly. Instead she said, "I was at the real estate office and I didn't see Heath there, only Beverly."

"My nephew doesn't go in much in the winter," Hamish admitted. "He's got a good head for business, but he doesn't have the hands-on work ethic of his father. I think my brother would be at his car dealership no matter what. I've known Argyll to open in the middle of a blizzard."

"So it's not strange that Heath wasn't there," Molly said.

"Not really, but it is odd that Loch Mallaig is in the middle of a burglary spree." Hamish scratched his beard thoughtfully. "If I was a burglar, I think I'd choose more lucrative shops to break into. At least the bookstore was off the beaten path, so it afforded the intruder privacy, but Lochside Realty and this place are right in the middle of things."

"Fergus pointed that out as well," Molly said. "Though I'm not sure it much matters this time of year."

"Fergus?" Laura's voice rose in a teasing emphasis. "So you chatted with Fergus?"

"He came by." Molly's cheeks warmed. Not for the first time she wished she didn't blush pink as a Valentine's rose every time her friends teased her. "He offered some security people from Castleglen if I was nervous being here alone."

"That's kind of him," Carol said. "Are you nervous being here alone? I could sleep over."

"Me too," Laura offered. "Sleepovers are fun."

"That does sound fun, but I am truly all right," Molly reassured her friends. "The burglar came and went, then moved on to the real estate office. I expect we're not on the agenda anymore." Though she did wonder who might still be on the list. If the burglaries were some kind of spree, what business would be hit next?

"Molly?" Bridget had appeared in the doorway. "Sorry to interrupt, but the woman you spoke to the other day is out front. She gave her name as Chelsea. If she is someone hoping to gossip, I need to borrow Hamish to send her on her way."

"Chelsea is not here to gossip, but you can definitely have Hamish back," Laura offered, receiving a glare and a grumble from him.

"Chelsea is Edgar Richardson's niece," Molly explained to Bridget. "I'll speak to her if you guys can spare me a little longer."

"No problem," Laura answered.

"Do what you can," Carol said. "That poor girl."

Molly walked out to the front area and saw Chelsea seated alone at a table near the counter, sipping what appeared to be hot chocolate. Her troubled face brightened when she saw Molly.

"Mrs. Ferris," Chelsea said, standing up as Molly joined her. "I'm sorry to bother you again."

"Call me Molly, please. You're not a bother. How can I help?"

Chelsea's smile grew brittle. "The police called me. They've released my uncle's shop. I've been trying to talk myself into going over there this afternoon, but I can't seem to make myself do it . . . at least not alone." Her eyes were beseeching. "You've been so kind, and I don't know anyone else in Loch Mallaig."

"Of course I'll go with you," Molly volunteered. "Will I be enough? It's possible Laura and Carol would come as well."

A smile played on Chelsea's lips. "We'd be quite a squad, wouldn't we? I'd hate to drag everyone into it, though. I'm sure I only need one person. Also, I don't really know the way. It gets dark so early here. I have a GPS in my rental car, but could I follow you there?"

"I can do even better than that," Molly said. "I'll drive both of us, if you want. Where are you staying?"

"Two Scots Guesthouse. They're so nice. I thought about asking

Mrs. Loganach, but I felt closer to you. I know that sounds silly since we only met once, but you spoke to my uncle and you clearly liked him."

"I'm happy to come," Molly said gently. "Would it be okay with you if I come and pick you up after we close?"

"Oh yes," Chelsea said readily. "Thank you so much. I can understand why my uncle wanted to retire here. This is such a kind town."

Molly would be inclined to agree, though she wasn't sure where the burglaries fit into that assessment. But she reasserted her promise to pick Chelsea up soon after the shop closed and got the younger woman's cell number to text her when she was on her way.

By the time Molly had helped with closing and taken Angus for another walk, the brief afternoon was already growing dark. She thought longingly of the coming spring when the predominant color in Loch Mallaig would be something other than gray. She appreciated all the red, pink, and white Valentine's decorations in the storefront windows for the burst of color if nothing else.

Since Molly had texted Chelsea before pulling out of her parking spot at Bread on Arrival, the young woman was watching for her through the front window at the guesthouse and promptly trotted out to meet her. Chelsea was well-bundled against the cold with a long wool coat and a thick scarf wrapped multiple times around her neck. She hopped into the Honda and greeted Molly in a slightly breathless tone, "Thank you again for coming with me."

"You're welcome," Molly said. "I should tell you that I have been to the bookstore since the burglary. The police asked Carol and me to let them know what had changed. It's a mess, but nothing that a few hours with a broom couldn't fix."

Chelsea sighed heavily. "I wish everything could be repaired so easily."

When they arrived at the farmhouse, Chelsea had a key to the front door, but nothing beyond that. She had no idea how to turn on the lights. In the late-day gloom, it took a little bit to find the switches by the glow of her cell phone. As soon as light flooded the entry, it became clear that despite Molly's effort to prepare Chelsea, the mess was shocking.

"Do you think my uncle was alive when the person did this?" Chelsea asked, her voice faint.

Molly shook her head sympathetically. "I honestly don't know."

Chelsea blinked rapidly. She put her hands over her face. "I'm not sure I should be here."

"If it's too soon, I can take you home." Molly put a gentle hand on the woman's shoulder. "We can come another time."

For a long moment neither of them spoke. Chelsea stood still, her hands over her face. Finally she dropped her hands. Her eyes were red, but dry. "Uncle Edgar must have seen so many terrible places during his work, places where terrible things happened. How do you suppose he got through it?"

"Maybe by concentrating on what he could do to help," Molly suggested.

Chelsea nodded. Her gaze swept the foyer. "Maybe we could clean up the broken stuff. It would be a start at least. It might be less overwhelming if we take this one step at a time."

"I think you're right. Let me see if I can find a broom." Molly left Chelsea in the foyer. She couldn't remember having seen a broom when she was in the shop previously, but there had to be one somewhere.

She reached the room with the checkout counter, where torn pieces of cardboard still covered the floor. She spotted a broom propped in the corner behind the counter. Molly picked her way carefully, not wanting to slip on the debris scattered on the floor. From the thick layer of broken pottery near the base of the counter, she suspected the intruder had specifically thrown some of the figurines against the side.

Molly slipped behind the register and reached for the broom. As she pulled the broom from the corner, the bristles caught on a gap in the counter that she hadn't noticed before. She squatted to untangle the broom, not wanting to accidentally yank out half the straw. As the broom slipped free, Molly caught a flash of something shiny in the gap. *What could that be?*

A chill crawled up her spine as she wondered if it was something worth killing for.

10

Intrigued, Molly set the broom down beside her and pulled out her phone, using the flashlight app to peer into the dark crevice. The glimmer turned out to be gold-leafed stripes on the spine of a book. Had the book fallen in and gotten caught like the broom while the intruder had scattered things in a frenzy? Molly squeezed her fingers into the gap, barely pinching the corner of the book. She pulled, wincing at the rough edge of the counter against her fingers.

"Molly?" Chelsea appeared in the doorway. The young woman appeared calmer. She had loosened her scarf and opened the front of her coat. She looked pointedly at Molly's hand in the gap, her expression curious.

"There's a book in here," Molly said as she slowly dragged it out. "I think it must have fallen in." She pulled the leather-bound book out into the light of the room. Aside from the gold leaf, the cover was plain. "How odd." Molly opened it up and her eyes went wide. The pages were filled with careful handwriting. "It's a journal of some kind."

"Is it my uncle's?" Chelsea asked.

"I don't know." Molly rose and held it out. "Is this his handwriting?"

"I only saw his handwriting a few times on those old birthday cards." Chelsea took the book and opened it in the middle. She scanned the page. "It could be his."

"Maybe the owner put his name in the front?" Molly suggested.

Chelsea flipped to the first page but shook her head. "It starts right in with dates and notes." She read silently for a moment, then she winced. "I think it is Uncle Edgar's journal. This seems to be about a case." She closed the cover and handed the book to Molly. "I don't want to read about police cases, at least not right now. Do you think you could read it and let me know if there's anything I should see?"

Molly was desperately curious to see what the book contained, but she did have some reservations. "Should we give this to the police? There may be a clue inside as to who might have meant him harm."

Chelsea shrugged. "Why don't you read it first, and if it seems to you that it's something they need to see, feel free to give it to them. Otherwise, I'm not sure they need the distraction. If it's nothing, I don't want to give them something that slows down the investigation."

That sounded reasonable, though Molly wasn't sure the police would agree. Still, her curiosity made her agree to the plan.

They stayed a few hours to tidy up the mess. Molly swept up broken pottery and filled one of the few intact packing boxes with the shards. Chelsea gathered scattered books into neat piles that she placed on bookshelves, then she picked up the bits of torn cardboard and made another pile for the trash. Finally, the worst of the mess was gone, though Molly suspected small bits of pottery would be found for a long time whenever furniture was moved in the house. Speaking of moving . . .

"What are you going to do with the bookstore?" she asked Chelsea as they donned their coats.

"I don't know," the young woman said. "I have a job and a house. I will probably sell it." She grimaced. "I feel guilty even saying that."

Molly tilted her head. "Why?"

"Uncle Edgar loved this place, even in the brief time he was here. It seems wrong to simply sell it."

"Maybe you can find a buyer who loves it every bit as much," Molly suggested.

Chelsea impulsively gave Molly a hug. "You're so good at making me feel better. Thank you." When she let Molly go, both women were surprised when Chelsea's stomach growled loudly. Chelsea pressed a hand to her stomach and giggled.

"Sounds as if you need some dinner," Molly said.

"I guess so. I haven't been eating much, but I feel so much better after being here with you. I think I'll see if Mrs. Loganach still has some of the soup she's been trying to feed me since I booked the room."

"It's sure to be tasty," Molly assured her. "Myra is an excellent cook."

"Want to join me?"

"I appreciate the invitation, but I think Angus would appreciate having me home. If you want to come back here another time and don't want to be alone, just call me." Molly held up the journal. "As soon as I know what's in here, I'll let you know." She tucked the journal inside her purse and fastened her coat buttons up to her neck.

Chelsea wrapped her thick scarf snugly around her neck again. "Sounds good."

Both women hunched their shoulders automatically as they stepped into the dark, frigid night and headed toward the lone car in the small parking lot. They'd nearly reached it when a man stepped out of the shadows with a huge dog by his side. His sudden appearance elicited a shriek from Chelsea.

"I'm sorry to startle you," Myron Webster said, though somehow Molly doubted the apology was sincere. "I saw you coming out of the house and thought I'd check who it was. I suppose Bernie and I are an unofficial neighborhood watch."

"Oh," Chelsea said, clearly still recovering.

"This is your uncle's neighbor," Molly offered by way of introduction. "Myron Webster."

"And Bernie," Myron said cheerfully, holding up the leash.

"How do you do," Chelsea said. Molly noticed she didn't offer her name, and she couldn't altogether blame the young woman. Myron did have an unnerving ability to appear in the darkness.

"I suppose you're in touch with the police," Myron said to Molly. "Have you heard anything about these burglaries? The whole neighborhood is jumpy."

"We don't know anything," Molly said. "And we need to get in out of the cold. It was nice to see you and Bernie again."

Molly hustled Chelsea the rest of the way to her car. When they hopped in, Molly peered through the windshield to see Myron and Bernie hadn't moved.

"Creepy guy," Chelsea muttered.

"Yeah, a little," Molly admitted as she started the car. "There are some eccentric characters in Loch Mallaig. Now you've met one, though he wouldn't have been my first choice."

"Lucky me," Chelsea said as Molly put the car in gear and left the man and dog behind.

When they reached the guesthouse, Chelsea reached out to touch Molly's arm. "I know I'm being stupid, but would you walk me in? I'm jumpy as a cat tonight, but I'm sure I'll be all right once I'm in my room."

"I thought you were going to ask Myra for some soup," Molly said.

"Maybe I'll go back down, but first I'm going to have the hottest bath I can stand. I'm freezing."

"Of course I'll see you in," Molly said. "You're in a strange town, and I can understand how unsettling everything has been."

The relief on Chelsea's face warmed Molly's heart. *Once a mom, always a mom*, Molly thought.

Two Scots Guesthouse was as quaint and neat as always, with several lights glowing cheerily. Molly wondered if Myra was in the kitchen.

Molly followed Chelsea up the stairs and to the first room at the top. "Thanks so much," Chelsea said as she unlocked the door with an old-fashioned key. "I know I'm being totally silly."

"You're being completely natural." Molly stepped into the room with Chelsea and surveyed the room. It was a pretty room with a charming handmade quilt on the antique iron bed. Molly noticed with approval that Chelsea wasn't one to leave clothes scattered around. "I don't see anything out of place."

But Chelsea stood frozen and staring at the old dresser that held a few bits of jewelry and other personal odds and ends. "You're wrong. Someone has been in here messing with my things."

"Are you sure?"

Chelsea's face was ghostly pale. "Dead sure."

Molly scanned the room in alarm. "Is something missing?" she asked. "Or simply moved? Maybe it was Myra. She may have dusted and brushed things a little."

"Nothing is missing." Chelsea pointed at the dresser. "But this earring is flipped over. I had them both lined up. I'm very careful about my things."

"That still sounds like something that could have happened during cleaning." Molly tried to voice her skepticism gently.

"But it was fine when I left with you," Chelsea insisted. "Myra did a housekeeping visit while I was out this morning. And you know there have been break-ins."

"Well, yes," Molly admitted, "but those had all the signs of a break-in. The doors were picked or windows broken and the burglars left a mess. But this room looks normal. Maybe check if anything is missing."

Chelsea peered into the dresser drawers and inside the closet. Then she peeked into the bathroom. Her firm expression had softened with what appeared to be doubt. "I can't tell if anything else was touched. But the earrings on the dresser aren't how I left them."

"Let's go downstairs and ask Myra," Molly suggested gently, sensing the younger woman's defensiveness and fear.

They found Myra in the kitchen, and she reacted with delight when Molly and Chelsea walked in. "Molly, how nice to see you. I didn't know you knew our guest."

"I'd met Chelsea's uncle," Molly said.

Myra nodded and gestured toward the kettle on the stove. "I was going to have a cup of herbal tea. Would you both join me? I have some shortbread too, straight from Bread on Arrival."

"I'd love some," Molly replied, thinking Angus could wait a little until Chelsea's fears were assuaged.

Myra examined Chelsea with concern. "You're pale. Have you eaten? I could fix you a chicken salad sandwich. I made some earlier with cranberries in it."

"That sounds good." Chelsea's voice was subdued, and Molly wondered if she was rethinking her belief that someone had disturbed her belongings.

"We were just upstairs," Molly said as she watched Myra bustling around. "Chelsea thought someone might have been in her room earlier."

Myra whirled around, her expression sheepish. "Oh dear, that would have been me. I peeked in to tidy up and do the bathrooms. This morning I was in such a rush after breakfast that I barely got the beds made. You'd think I wouldn't get behind with only two guests, but somehow I managed."

"Oh," Chelsea said, the word barely more than a breath. The relief on her face was plain. "I'm glad it was you. I've been silly, and Molly is kind to humor me. I guess it's being in a strange place, and with my uncle's death . . ."

Myra patted the younger woman's arm. "Don't fret about it.

I'm only sorry to have caused you concern. Now, let me get you that sandwich. Everything is easier with a full tummy."

Molly let Myra coax her into a sandwich as well, and they purposefully talked about pleasant topics while they sipped chamomile tea and ate. Myra asked Molly about how she was coming along with her bagpiping, which clearly astounded Chelsea.

"I guess I always picture men in kilts with bagpipes, not women," Chelsea said. "Is it difficult?"

"It's not the easiest instrument to play," Molly admitted. "But I love it. The sound transports the hearer."

"That's true enough," Myra said. "You should hear The Piping Yoopers when they're all together. It's amazing."

Chelsea smiled. "I'd enjoy that."

When Molly finally left, Chelsea was still chatting happily with Myra. The young woman's color was normal again, and the stress lines gone from her face. Molly felt sure she'd left Chelsea in good hands.

When she reached Bread on Arrival, Angus was in the yard waiting for her. She walked him up to the apartment and gave him a treat to ease her guilt at leaving him alone. He gobbled the cookie happily enough, but then he raced over to the hook where his leash hung. He began jumping, clearly trying to catch the leash.

"You're as subtle as a sledgehammer," Molly informed him as she removed Edgar's journal from her purse. "And you were outside a minute ago."

Angus simply ignored her and continued trying to grab the leash. Molly sighed and placed the book on a side table before taking the leash down.

"A *short* walk," she insisted, hooking the leash to the wriggling dog. "Then I'm going to take a hot bath and spend some time reading."

Angus was so happy to be on the leash that he didn't even react to the dreaded word "bath." In fact, he didn't even complain when Molly strapped his cute plaid jacket on him. "You'll be happy for it outside," she told him. "It's gotten bitter."

She gave her warm apartment a last longing gaze before she headed out. The night was fully upon them, making the cold feel even deeper than before. Molly hoped it wouldn't take long to wear Angus out enough to appreciate a quiet night indoors.

The happy little dog seemed oblivious to the weather, though, instead taking a ridiculous amount of pleasure from leaping off the sidewalk into piles of snow, nearly disappearing more than once. The vanishing trick made Molly laugh, especially since it seemed to clearly bring Angus so much joy. They walked into Dumfries Park, which was utterly silent and still except for the sound of the lapping water of Loch Mallaig. Though Molly couldn't help but enjoy the beauty of the park, the icy chill coming from the water seemed to slip right through her heavy coat and sink into her bones.

She was grateful when Angus showed signs of being tired of his game. He stopped rushing from the paved path, and Molly started toward home. She soon saw she'd overestimated the little dog's energy when he sat down in the path and refused to budge.

"Wore yourself out, did you?" she teased him.

Angus had nothing to say to that, but he stared up at her pointedly.

"Okay, I'll carry you." She bent and picked him up. Molly could feel right through her gloves that his paws were cold and still a bit damp from his snow jumping. She was glad she'd put a warm jacket on him. "Maybe I should get you some boots."

As she pressed the dog against her, she thought of the hot bath and reading she had planned for the evening. She hoped the journal wasn't full of graphic details of Edgar Richardson's time on the police force. That kind of reading wouldn't do anything for her nerves. Still, maybe there would be references to anyone Ed considered a threat. Molly pushed aside the thought for the moment, not wanting it to ruin what had been an almost meditative and certainly refreshing walk.

Part of Molly wanted to linger in the park despite the cold. It was incredibly beautiful when it was so still. She loved that about winter. It seemed to hush the entire world, at least at night. But the cold finally won, and she decided it was time to head in. With a huff that created a cloud of faint steam about her face, she walked toward the bakehouse with Angus in her arms.

By the time Molly reached the sidewalk, Angus was sound asleep in her arms. The little dog felt heavier with every step. She'd be happy to reach home and put him down. She picked up her pace to reach the fenced yard and the stairs up to her apartment.

She'd barely stepped into the shadow cast by the Victorian house when someone emerged from the darkness. Molly was fairly sure it was a man, though she couldn't see his face. He wore a hat pulled low, and most of his face was covered by a scarf.

"I'm sorry, we're closed. Can I help you?" she asked.

Instead of answering, the man rushed at her and grabbed hold of Angus. He was trying to kidnap her dog!

11

With a yelp of alarm, Molly tightened her grip on Angus. "Leave him alone!"

Molly's shout cut through Angus's exhaustion, and he clearly did not appreciate being grabbed by a stranger. With a snarl, Angus sank his teeth deep in the man's gloved hand. The gloves must not have offered much protection because the man roared with pain, let go, and ran.

Angus barked wildly as the man ran out of the yard. Molly wrapped her arms tight around her dog and backed up against the rear entrance to the bakehouse. She fumbled for her keys and let herself in, eager to put a solid door between herself and a dognapper.

Once inside, Molly set a squirming Angus down and began flipping on lights throughout the first floor. She couldn't stand the thought of being in the dark, not even for a moment.

As soon as all the downstairs lights were on, Molly called Angus over to her. She ran her hands gently over his sides. "Are you all right? Did that awful man hurt you?"

Angus didn't appear to be injured, though he quickly grew tired of the examination and dashed off, enjoying his rare access to the bakehouse. Molly's gaze was drawn to the bakery's windows. The dark pressed against them, broken only by the glow of streetlamps that seemed entirely too distant.

With shaking hands, Molly pulled her phone from her coat pocket. She wasn't sure who to call. Would the police be interested in someone trying to grab her dog? Would Angus biting him be considered an attack?

Finally she decided that what she wanted to do was hear the voice of a friend. She called Fergus and quickly explained what had happened.

"I'm on my way over," Fergus said without hesitation.

Guilt washed over Molly and she sat shakily in one of the customer chairs. "You don't have to do that. I wasn't looking for a rescue. I'm safely in the bakehouse. I mostly wanted to tell someone, and I'm not sure if I should report it to the police."

"With the burglaries and the murder, the police do have a lot on their plate," Fergus said reluctantly. "But I don't think you should be there alone."

Molly managed a weak chuckle. "Fergus, I'm here alone every night. That's what being single means. Besides, I have Angus." At the sound of his name, Angus trotted over and sat at her feet.

"I'll tell you this much," Fergus said. "I'm glad he bit the guy."

Molly leaned forward to rub Angus's ears. "Normally he's not a biter and I'm glad, but on this occasion, I prefer it to the alternative of losing him. Why on earth would someone try to grab Angus?"

"He is a purebred Scottie, and it shows," Fergus replied musingly. "Purebred dogs are valuable."

"I suppose." Molly wasn't convinced, but she didn't see how arguing the point would help. "I think I'll call Greer tomorrow and let her know what happened. She can help me decide if it's something that should have a formal report. With so many weird things going on around town, I expect this will just give them one more thing to file away."

"I'd feel better if you would let me come over and hang out for a while," Fergus said.

"I appreciate the offer, but I think I'm ready for some quiet time with Angus."

"Okay, if that's what you want. Maybe try writing down an account of what happened. Sometimes you can recall small details when you do that. For instance, ask yourself what made you think the person was a man."

"I suppose it may not have been." Molly frowned, thinking back. "I didn't see his face and he wasn't tall. But it sounded like he had a man's voice. He yelled when Angus bit him."

"That's not always a guarantee, but it's a good start," Fergus said. "It could be that there's another detail that you noticed without realizing it."

Molly chuckled wanly. "That sounds mysterious."

"The human mind is mysterious. And yours probably more than most."

Molly couldn't miss the teasing tone in that last remark. "You keep making fun of me and I won't tell you about the other thing that happened tonight."

"Molly Ferris, you're going to be the death of me," he said, the jesting tone replaced by exasperation. "What happened? A death threat? Or did you find a body?"

"Nothing like that, thank you." She explained about Ed's journal, adding, "I'm going to give it to the police tomorrow. I think they should at least know it exists, whether they want to dig through it or not."

"I guess that's okay," he said. "As long as you keep me up to date on what you find tonight when you're reading it, which I'm sure you will."

Sometimes he knew her too well. "Okay, I'll report on it tomorrow," Molly promised. "You've made me feel much better. I'm going to get off the phone now and head up with Angus."

"Please send me a text when you're upstairs and you've checked all the windows and doors."

"I will," she said, then thanked him for helping her calm down before ending the call. All the doors and windows were locked and secure, so Molly and Angus headed upstairs. Angus rallied enough to gobble down some kibble before settling on the rug in the sitting room. He fell asleep in moments, complete with snoring. Molly was always amazed that such a small creature could manage such loud sounds.

She curled up on the sofa with the journal she'd found at the bookstore and pulled a knitted afghan over her lap. It had been a gift from Carol years before, and that fact made her feel even more secure, as if her friend were here now to comfort her.

Molly knew reading the journal of a murder victim would not be the most soothing way to end the day, but she didn't want to hold on to the potential evidence any longer than necessary. Realistically, she needed to tell Greer about it when she called to report the attempted dognapping.

While she read, Molly rarely spent much time puzzling over words thanks to Ed's neat handwriting. It quickly became clear that the retired policeman used the journal to sum up his thoughts at the end of each day. The earliest entry was from a little over a year before, and the most recent had been written the day before the man's death. Molly decided to read backward from the last entry.

She immediately found Ed's viewpoint engaging.

Myron and Bernie have passed by for their nightly glare at the shop, he wrote in the last entry.

> *I'm tempted to leave dog biscuits for Bernie, but Myron would probably explode at the idea of my buying the dog's affections.*

Molly suspected Ed was right about that. Nothing else interesting was noted for the day, so she flipped the page to the day before. She learned that Ed had gotten a call about the books he'd bought from the Emily Finch estate. Molly sat up straighter as she read.

The guy offered me twice what I paid and probably more than I'll get selling the items piecemeal. I've barely poked around in the first box, but everything inside seems to be cheap and cheesy. I should have jumped at the offer. What is it about me and mysteries? If someone offers a lot of money, there's even more money somewhere. That's what police work taught me. I hope I don't turn out to be an idiot who passed up a golden goose egg.

Molly stared at the page, wondering if the caller could have been after the jewelry Mrs. Finch was supposed to have owned. Since Edgar wouldn't sell the boxes, had the caller decided to take matters into his own hands and break into the bookstore? It certainly made sense, which meant that caller was probably responsible for Edgar's death. According to Beverly, Sean Mitchum had been furious about the missing jewelry. Could he have figured out that the fortune he expected could be sitting at a used bookstore?

Valentine's Day had technically arrived when Molly woke to the cruel insistence of her alarm clock. True daylight wouldn't arrive for a while, though, and every part of her body urged her to switch off the alarm and go back to sleep.

Instead, she sat up and swung her legs over the side of the bed while she waited for the rest of her body to catch up to the plan. She had a vague, nagging headache that she suspected came from a night filled with dreams of dark figures lurking in the shadows. In the dreams, Molly was certain she was catching glimpses of the burglar, but though she chased the flitting figure, she could never catch up enough to truly see the person.

Molly rubbed her face. "I hope things improve from here."

Angus romped across the bed and nestled in Molly's lap. She gave him a squeeze. "That journal freaked me out, Angus." He laid the side of his head against her hand, making her smile. "All right. I suppose we should get this day rolling."

When she finished getting ready, Molly wandered through the apartment with her coffee mug in her hand, hoping the movement would help clear the last of the cobwebs out of her head. She passed the office door and, as she glimpsed the computer, she realized with a start that there was someone she'd completely forgotten to investigate: Emily Finch's nurse.

For a moment, Molly couldn't come up with the woman's name, though she recalled Beverly having the same problem. She sat down in the desk chair and mentally ran through her conversation with Beverly. The name popped into her head. "Ida Paterson," she said aloud. "And Helping Hearts Health Care."

She typed the nurse's name into the search engine first, and a wealth of hits came back. She clicked a few, hoping to luck into finding the nurse easily. She found an Ida Paterson who was on a city council in Vermont, an Ida Paterson who groomed dogs in Virginia, and an Ida Paterson who was a police officer in Arizona. With a soft groan, Molly realized she could probably do this all day. She needed to approach the search from a different direction.

She typed in *Helping Hearts Health Care Loch Mallaig* and found the website. The link for staff was right on the first page. "There we go," she murmured. But when she clicked the link, she quickly found that Ida Paterson was not in the list of visiting nurses. She sighed, her hope deflating like a burst balloon. "So much for that."

Molly sat back in the chair and tapped her chin, trying to come up with another way to approach the search. She searched for visiting nurses in Loch Mallaig and found the second company Beverly had mentioned, Traveling Care. She quickly found Ida Paterson wasn't on their roster either.

It wasn't until she widened her search to visiting nurses in the whole state that she finally found Ida Paterson on a list for a company out of Copper Harbor. With a rush of victory, Molly clicked on the woman's name and brought up a short biography and photo. She studied Ida Paterson's face. The handsome woman wore a serious expression made more severe by the salt-and-pepper hair pulled into a tight bun. The short biography mentioned that she was the newest nurse in the practice, so Molly guessed she'd moved to Copper Harbor sometime after Emily's death.

"But what did I learn?" Molly saw no reason to imagine this nurse as a burglar or a dognapper. With a sigh, she abandoned her search, checked for new online orders for the bakehouse, and printed off information for the day's shipments.

After drinking enough coffee to feel human again, Molly headed downstairs. She could already hear sounds from the kitchen and knew she wasn't the first to work. As she rounded the corner into the kitchen she was greeted warmly by both Laura and Carol, who were carrying ingredients to begin their morning baking.

"Happy Valentine's Day," Carol sang out.

"Bah humbug," Laura said cheerfully, "but good morning." She set the brick of butter she carried at her workspace and peered into Molly's face. "You're looking a little rough."

"Thanks, friend," Molly said wryly. "I was hoping the makeup would hide it. I didn't sleep great."

"No wonder." Carol aimed a knowing gaze at Laura. "I told you we should have had a sleepover."

"We tried," Laura said. "We could have come back after your time with Chelsea, Molly."

"I didn't need a sleepover," Molly insisted, though it might have made her evening a little less eventful.

"So you say," Carol replied, but then she shifted subjects. "How was your visit with Chelsea?"

For a moment Molly didn't respond, feeling overwhelmed. So much had happened, and her friends didn't even know about the attempted dognapping. Wearily, she realized she wanted to put off telling them for a little while longer. "Shouldn't I go prep for opening?" Molly asked, waving a hand toward the customer area.

"Don't tease," Carol insisted as she dumped a scoop of flour into a mixing bowl. "We want to know if you learned anything from Chelsea."

Molly dropped her hand. "We found Ed's journal hidden in the counter at the bookstore," she said. "Chelsea told me to read it before giving it to the police. It doesn't point to an obvious killer, but Ed did note that someone had called and tried to buy all the items he'd gotten from the estate sale—for twice what he paid."

Laura began unwrapping the butter. "That is curious. Did he say the name of the person who called?"

"No, but I wonder if it was Emily's grandson, Sean Mitchum," Molly replied. "Beverly said he was upset that his grandmother's things were sold before he had a chance to examine them."

"If it was him," Carol said, "it would make him a strong suspect for the break-ins. He's searching for whatever he thinks his grandmother had."

"But would he kill for it?" Laura asked, her tone doubtful. "I know Edgar died of a heart attack, but if he's the one who broke in here, he threw a knife at Molly's head."

"Money is a major motive for murder," Carol replied. "In books and movies anyway." She ticked off her fingers. "There's also revenge, passion, or blackmail—though I've often wondered how much blackmail really goes on in the world."

Laura snorted. "Well, since movies also regularly feature cartoon birds helping princesses clean their castles, I imagine the incidents of blackmail could be a little inflated."

"Could be." Molly took a breath. "Not to change the subject, but something weird happened last night. I still need to call Greer about it, but I should tell you both."

"Weird?" Carol and Laura spoke in unison with identical expressions of keen interest on their faces.

Molly explained about how she was carrying Angus home when someone came out of the shadows and tried to grab him. "If I hadn't had such a good grip on him, I don't know what would have happened. As it was, Angus didn't appreciate the rough handling and bit the guy."

Carol raised a hand to her mouth. "Oh, Molly, how terrifying for you. Is Angus all right?"

"He's perfectly fine. But I locked the doggy door today so he can't get out to the fenced yard. I'll need to walk him more, but I couldn't bear the thought of him out in the yard with no one watching in case the guy came back."

"That sounds wise," Laura agreed. "And don't worry about the extra walks. You do whatever you need to keep Angus safe. We all love the little fella."

"Definitely," Carol agreed.

Molly's eyes stung. She was touched by the rousing show of support. It shouldn't have surprised her. Carol and Laura were like sisters to her, but after the hard night, she was especially grateful for their kindness.

"I don't know what's happening in this town," Carol said as she returned to dumping ingredients in her mixing bowl. "Someone breaks into a bookstore, which maybe makes sense if it's that Sean person. And maybe the real estate office for the same person, but why here?

What do we have to do with any of this? And why try to grab Angus? The whole thing is absurd."

"And who steals a dog by snatching it from the owner's arms?" Molly added as a rush of anger at the man surged through her. "A dog bite is the logical result of that. I hope it hurt."

Laura raised an eyebrow at Molly's outburst. "Maybe the attempted break-in here isn't related to the others," she suggested, clearly switching gears to calm her friend. "And the dognapping too. Coincidences do happen."

"That many?" Carol asked.

Molly thought Laura could be right, though she did find it odd that the break-ins at the real estate office and the bakehouse had been done by someone with poor lock-picking skills, at least according to the police. Nothing made sense about the last few days. "Why not go after targets that are more likely to have valuables and money? Even Happily Ever Efter or Thistle and That seem a better target for small valuables that a thief could easily carry. They both have some costume jewelry that is not exactly cheap."

"Maybe the burglar is choosing places that are less secure," Laura suggested.

"And we're less secure than the bridal boutique or the gift shop?" Molly asked. "Plus, the intruder didn't give up when he found the lock at the real estate office was too hard to pick. He simply broke the glass. That makes this feel targeted."

"I can understand choosing us, at least somewhat," Carol admitted. "Being right next to the park does make us seem a little more secluded."

Molly sighed deeply, trying not to think about how her apartment was included in that description. "Honestly, I'll feel better if I get to work. I'm going to call Greer later, but for now, I want to be up to my elbows in flour. Is there anything on the plan that's safe to hand over to me?"

"Of course." Again Laura and Carol spoke together before scolding Molly about not believing in her own baking skills. It was a scolding Molly had heard enough to make it comforting.

With Angus shut in upstairs, Molly worried about getting too busy to remember to walk him, but the little dog made sure she didn't forget. He helpfully broke into a flurry of barking every few hours to inspire a walk. It was on the way back from a midmorning romp around the park that Molly spotted a familiar Range Rover Sport in the Bread on Arrival parking lot. She peered through the bakehouse's front door and spotted the vehicle's owner chatting with Bridget.

Bridget noticed Molly immediately and said something to Fergus, who turned. His face lit up, and he came out to meet her.

"Fergus," Molly greeted him. "Happy Valentine's Day."

"Same to you," he said. "I was trying to talk my way past Bridget so I could see you."

"And here I am," Molly said. "But I'm headed upstairs since I can't have Angus in here. He's not exactly a service dog."

"Though he did a good service last night," Fergus said as he bent and patted the little dog on the head.

"Hero or not, he's headed upstairs," Molly said. "Would you like to join me? I could do with a cup of tea and a sit down."

Fergus quickly agreed, and Molly led him to the outer staircase to her apartment. As she entered the hallway, she texted Carol that she was back. *I'm going to have a chat with Fergus, but I'll be down shortly.*

Take your time! Carol replied as Molly had expected. Her friends tended to be enthusiastic about any time she spent with Fergus. She knew they were matchmaking a bit, but since they rarely got pushy, she mostly pretended not to notice.

As soon as Molly had made tea, she and Fergus settled down at the table next to the kitchenette window. Molly loved the view it gave her of Loch Mallaig. She took a long sip of her tea, enjoying the warmth after the chilly walk outside. "I'm surprised you're away from Castleglen today," she said to Fergus. "Don't you have a fancy dinner tonight?"

"Medium fancy," he answered. "But it doesn't require much prep from me. As you probably remember, Neil insisted we ought to have dancing too. He's moved some tables around at King's Heid Pub for the evening. We'll see how it goes."

"Well, I'm sure you're still playing hooky when you could be there, and I'm touched you're doing it for me."

"For you and Angus," Fergus said. "As you know, that little guy has stolen my heart."

Molly laughed. "He's a bit annoyed today because I won't let him outside without me. I can't handle the stress."

"Have you spoken to the police?"

"Not yet, but I'm planning to call Greer." Molly set down her mug and sighed. "I've been putting it off. I'll need to hand over Ed's journal too, and I wish I had more time with it. I read a good bit last night and skimmed the rest, but I might have missed something."

"If you did, the police will find it. That's their job." Fergus glanced at the clock on the wall. "I have to run. I'm letting Neil handle the whole Valentine's deal, but I should probably make sure he hasn't hit any problems."

Molly led Fergus down the stairs and out into the customer area since his car was parked out front. They'd barely reached the café when Officer Drummond walked in. Fergus nodded toward the officer, giving Molly a pointed look. "I know, I know," she said with a sigh. "Officer Drummond, can I speak to you?"

Dismay crossed his face. "Are you about to ruin my Valentine's Day? Am I going to regret wanting a scone for breakfast?"

"Certainly not," Molly said. "I just want to tell you something that happened last night. I'll give you the scone on the house for listening."

Drummond perked up. "Then I'm all ears."

"And I'm out of here," Fergus said. "See you, Molly. Happy Valentine's Day."

Molly collected a cinnamon scone and a coffee. She brought the bribes to the corner table where the police officer had already shucked off his warm jacket and chosen a seat. Molly slipped into the chair across from him as she set the goodies down.

"Can I eat while you talk?" he asked hopefully.

"Of course." She launched into a description of the near dognapping and was pleased to see Drummond quickly lose interest in his scone.

"Is Angus all right?" he asked.

"No sign of any injury, but it scared me."

"I can imagine. Can you describe the person?"

Molly shrugged. "I think it was a man, but it was dark and it happened fast. Plus, the person had his face covered. I was mostly worried about Angus. I honestly don't expect you to do anything about it, but Fergus thought it best if I let the police know."

He took a sip of his coffee and nodded. "It's strange. Not that Angus isn't a great pup, but it's not like he's won dog shows. Around here, purebred Scotties sometimes end up in rescues when people find out they can have a rather challenging temperament. That means there's not much market for them."

"Well, the person last night certainly wanted Angus," Molly said.

"I'll ask the chief to assign a patrol to cruise by here a few times each night to keep any other weird incidents at bay. And you should avoid letting Angus out unattended."

"I'm already on that," Molly assured him. She let the officer have a couple bites of his scone while she tried to figure out a way to bring up the journal without getting a serious lecture about withholding evidence. She wished it was Greer across from her. Not that Greer wouldn't scold her as well, but Molly was closer to the younger officer and wouldn't mind the rebuke so much.

As if her thoughts had somehow conjured her friend, the bakehouse door swung open and Greer rushed in, her cheeks and nose pink from the cold. "Drummond, we have to go."

"What's up?" he asked as he rose from the chair.

"There's been another call out near the bookstore," Greer said. "An attack. Someone may have been killed."

12

"An attack?" Molly echoed, her voice thin and high. She even felt a little dizzy and didn't dare stand. Her brain flashed a mental image of Chelsea lying in the snow. *Why would she go to the house alone?* She covered her mouth in horror. *Because I showed her it was safe.*

Greer's next words eased her mind slightly. "The guy is down, but no one can get to him to help. His dog is standing over the body and won't let anyone near it."

In an instant, Molly realized the victim must be Myron. It made sense, she supposed. His neighborhood patrols with Bernie frequently brought him near the bookstore.

"If you're talking about Myron and Bernie," Molly said urgently, finally standing, "I know that dog. I've interacted with him and petted him. And he loves Angus. Maybe if I come and bring Angus, Bernie will let us help Myron."

Though Greer's expression lightened at Molly's suggestion, the other officer was clearly less enthusiastic.

"Just what we need," Drummond said as he shrugged into his jacket. "More dogs."

"It could be our only solution," Greer said. "We need to get the man some help." She nodded to Molly. "Go get Angus."

Molly raced into the kitchen, sparing only the briefest of explanations to Carol and Laura before hurrying upstairs to collect Angus.

After a tense drive to the bookstore, Molly followed the police officers behind the old farmhouse. As she circled the house, she wondered what Myron and Bernie were doing in the backyard. Surely his dog walking didn't take him through the yards of his neighbors.

Leggy, overgrown plantings peeked out from beneath mounds of snow here and there, suggesting the old house hadn't had the attention it needed in the days before the sale. A ridiculous thought passed through Molly's head as she wondered if Edgar had been interested in gardening. *What difference does that make now?* But Molly suspected she was simply trying not to see what lay before her.

On the snowy patio space not far from the door, Myron lay crumpled and still. Molly saw no sign of blood, but the man wasn't moving and the huge dog stood over him, growling deep in his chest at the officers and medical technicians nearby. A pair of animal control officers stood close with poles and loops, but from the glances they exchanged, they weren't exactly excited at the thought of taking on a dog that size. And pulling Bernie away without hurting Myron more would only complicate the procedure.

Molly crept closer with Angus in her arms. Angus barked sharply at his big friend, and Bernie's head swung around so quickly that his large, hairy ear hit him in the nose.

"Hi Bernie," Molly said in a soothing voice. "Do you remember us?" Bernie stood still as a statue, but he had stopped growling.

Angus whined and wriggled, clearly wanting to get down and greet his friend, but Molly didn't intend to allow that until she was sure the big dog wouldn't attack.

"Bernie," Molly said, patting her thigh with one hand. "Come here, Bernie. Come see Angus."

At first, Molly worried that she'd come for nothing as Bernie simply stared in her direction. Then, slowly, the big dog's tail swung back and forth. He continued to peer toward Molly, and it was clear he recognized her or Angus or both.

"Come on, Bernie. It's okay. Come here." Molly patted her leg again. Bernie took one step toward Molly, and one of the animal control officers moved closer. At the sound of the man's boot on the patio, Bernie swung his head toward him and growled again.

Molly addressed Greer, who appeared to be holding her breath. "If everyone backs up out of Bernie's line of sight, I think I can get him to come to me. Please, can I try?"

"You've done better than anyone else so far," Greer said, then began ordering the animal control people back. The other police officers edged away as well. The ambulance crew finally joined them, but their reluctance was clear on their faces. They needed to get to Myron, and they knew it. They were losing precious minutes that could make the difference between life and death for him.

"Bernie," Molly said, making her voice a bit more commanding, the kind of tone she would take with Angus when she needed him to obey. "Bernie, come."

The dog offered her a longer gaze before he dropped his head and licked Myron's hand, whining softly.

"I know, Bernie. Come here and let us help Myron. No one here will hurt him." Deciding it was time for Angus to get his wish, she set him on the ground, and the little dog rushed to his friend.

The two dogs sniffed noses and wagged their tails. Molly called them again and they both trotted toward her. As soon as Bernie reached her, she buried her hands in his thick fur, searching for his collar as she told him over and over what a good boy he was. When she found the collar, she slipped her hand through it. She didn't know if she could hold Bernie if he decided he still needed to protect Myron, but she intended to try.

As Molly continued to edge backward with the two dogs, the ambulance crew moved in on Myron quickly and quietly, careful not to draw Bernie's attention again. Finally Molly felt she'd gained enough distance from Myron and dared to continue feeling her way around the leather collar with her hands until she found the trailing leash. She wrapped it around her hand. "Do you want a treat?"

Clearly Bernie understood the magic word every bit as well as Angus. The big dog's tail wagged slowly as Molly led him still farther from his master's body. She stopped when they were close to the edge of the patio, then rooted in her purse and came up with a few of the small dog biscuits she normally gave Angus. She gave all but one of them to Bernie, eliciting an annoyed yip from Angus. Bernie responded to Angus's bark with one of his own—a deep, menacing sound, but one accompanied by tail wags. Molly handed Angus his biscuit, then glanced at the attendants kneeling by Myron.

To her shaky relief, she saw Myron's hand move. It was only a twitch, but the sight of it made Molly's eyes fill with tears of relief. He was alive. Bernie's big head nudged Molly's hand and he whined. "It's going to be all right," she told him as she stroked his fuzzy ears. "Everything's going to be all right."

To Molly's surprise, she spotted Fergus walking around the end of the building, followed by Chelsea Lowell. "I thought you were going back to Castleglen, Fergus," Molly said. "And Chelsea, what are you doing here?"

"We met at the road," Chelsea said, gesturing behind her. "The police called me because I'm the owner of this property now."

"And I heard on the gossip vine that the police were out here," Fergus said. "I called the bakehouse to see if anyone knew anything. Bridget told me you were here."

"Loch Mallaig's news network is so efficient," Molly said, rolling her eyes.

Fergus nodded at the crowd of people around Myron. "How is he? Do you know what happened?"

"He's alive," Molly replied. "Beyond that I don't know much of anything."

"Why are terrible things happening on this property?" Chelsea asked as she wrapped her arms around herself. "My uncle wanted a quiet life surrounded by books. Why has everything gone so wrong?"

Molly looked sympathetically at Chelsea's tear-filled eyes, but she didn't have an answer for her. Instead, she simply put an arm around the young woman's shaking shoulders. The dogs must have recognized Chelsea's distress as well. Both leaned against her legs, and Bernie pushed his huge head under Chelsea's hand. Molly was impressed by the dog's concern for a distressed human when he was so worried about his own master.

Chelsea rubbed Bernie's ears. "I'm sorry. It's all been a bit much."

"Nothing to be sorry about," Fergus assured her. "I can only say that the police will sort this out eventually. I'm certain of it."

"But why was that man even here?" Chelsea asked. "Why would he walk his dog in my uncle's backyard? I wouldn't mind, but clearly it wasn't safe for him."

As Chelsea was echoing Molly's own question, she offered one suggestion. "Your uncle said that Myron and Bernie passed this property often. In his journal, he called it their patrol. Maybe they were patrolling and saw someone on the property. Myron probably approached the person to ask what they were doing here and was attacked."

"Are you sure he was attacked?" Fergus asked. "I don't see any blood."

"Greer called it an attack when she told Michael Drummond," Molly said. "I don't know what that was based on."

"He has a knot on his head," Greer said, walking over from the group attending to Myron. "Molly, the ambulance crew is ready to load

Mr. Webster onto the gurney and requested that you make sure the dog is distracted. Also, the animal control guys asked me if you could help them get the dog in the van. He might go easier for you than for them."

"It will take all of us to keep him distracted." Molly decided not to address the second request and merely put a hand on the big dog's head. Bernie's focus was on her immediately. Fergus and Chelsea joined in, loading attention on the dog while the ambulance crew quickly slid Myron onto the gurney and wheeled him out of the backyard. If Bernie saw what was happening, he didn't react to it.

Molly dreaded the idea of sending Bernie to a temporary shelter. She knew they'd take good care of him, but surely it would only traumatize the dog further. One of the animal control officers walked over to join them and Bernie huddled against Molly, clearly uncomfortable with so many strangers. "I hate to send Bernie away. Maybe I should take him home with me until Myron is out of the hospital."

Fergus patted the dog on the head. "Are you sure you have enough apartment for that? Any room he enters won't have space for you in it. And if he gets down into the bakehouse, we'll have a new saying to replace bull in a china shop—Bernie in a bakery."

Molly raised her chin. "I'm sure he'd be a perfect gentleman. Plus, Laura and Carol would never want me to abandon a brave, loyal dog like Bernie. He may have been a problem a few minutes ago, but he was only trying to keep Myron safe."

"The ambulance attendants said he also must have helped keep his master warm," Greer added. "The victim would have been in far worse shape if he'd been exposed to the elements for long."

"See?" Molly raised eyebrows at Fergus. "He's a hero. A hero deserves better than to be in a shelter, even if it would only be temporary." She didn't quite know how cohabitating with the huge dog would work in her apartment, but she would figure it out.

"I could take the dog," Chelsea suggested. "He's awfully sweet, and there's a sign at Two Scots Guesthouse that says they're pet friendly."

Greer grimaced. "I'm not sure they're *that* friendly. You take that beast into the guesthouse and Myra is going to faint. If Molly's apartment isn't big enough, a guestroom certainly won't be."

Chelsea raised her chin and Molly was glad to see the young woman seemed to have shaken off some of the shock she'd shown earlier. "Mrs. Loganach is very kind. I think she'd want to help."

"It's not a fair position to put her in," Greer insisted. "Honestly, the shelter isn't bad. It's clean and warm."

"And full of strangers." Molly resisted the urge to stamp her foot, but she wasn't giving up. Like Chelsea, she felt almost irrationally dedicated to this cause. She couldn't help Myron right now, but she could keep Bernie out of the shelter.

"If it means that much to you, I can take him home with me," Fergus offered. "My place is certainly big enough, and having this giant dog around will make it feel less cavernous." He gazed into Bernie's warm, brown eyes. "What do you say? Want to be pals?" The big dog rubbed his head against Fergus's hand in a friendly way.

"Well, if Bernie's on board, I'm grateful," Molly said. "It sounds like a reasonable solution."

"I suppose," Chelsea said, though she sounded more disappointed than relieved.

"You'll have to sign a form," the animal control officer said. "But we don't mind not having to wrestle him into the van."

"Sounds like a win all around," Fergus said. "If we're done here, I'll sign the paper and take Bernie home to get settled. Then maybe I'll go in to work for a little while." He grinned. "Though this has been a great way to avoid Valentine's Day."

As Fergus led the dog away, Molly groaned quietly. "I should head to work myself. Greer, do you suppose you could let me know how Myron is once you get an update?"

"I can manage that," Greer said distractedly. Her gaze was on Officer Drummond, who was examining the ground where Myron had been sprawled only minutes earlier.

"Molly?" Chelsea put a hand lightly on Molly's arm. "What you said about the injured man having potentially confronted a trespasser makes me wonder if I should go inside and check on the house. Could you come with me?" She offered an embarrassed smile. "I know the guy must be long gone, but I'll feel better if I'm not alone."

This brought Greer's attention to them. "Checking on the property is a good idea," she said. "I'll come too."

Chelsea pulled out her keys as they walked to the back door, but when they reached it, all three of them froze. The door was slightly ajar. "I'm sure this was locked after we left," Chelsea whispered. "I was careful about locking up after someone had already broken in here once."

"Then you'd better let me go in first and sweep the place. Wait until I give the all clear." Greer pulled on gloves, then nudged the door open with her elbow and peeked inside. She held up a hand to wait and walked into the farmhouse mudroom. Moments later, Molly and Chelsea heard her shriek.

They exchanged a glance, then charged into the house.

Greer stood in the middle of the mudroom, staring at the wall. Someone had left a message on the wall in dripping, blood-red letters.

I will have what's mine!

13

The women were silent for a long, shocked moment.

Finally Greer said, "What are you two doing in here? I told you to wait."

"We thought you might be in trouble," Molly protested.

"And two unarmed women would have done what, exactly?" Greer demanded. "Go back outside and let me finish my sweep."

"No," Chelsea said stubbornly. "We were in the house last, so we'll be the best to spot anything out of place. Like, say, a terrifying message written in blood."

"Besides," Molly added, "if anyone was still here, they probably fled when you yelled, and you've got more backup right outside."

Greer glared at Molly and Chelsea, then threw up her arms in resignation. "All right, all right. You can both come along. But you stay behind me in case anyone is hiding somewhere."

"Now, how about the blood message? What does it mean?" Chelsea asked. She stood with her head averted to avoid reading it again.

Molly peered at the letters. "I don't think it's blood."

Greer stepped up on a mudroom bench, bringing her even with the words. She leaned close and sniffed, then hopped back down. "It's red paint."

Chelsea folded her arms over her chest. "And that makes it all right?"

"Nothing about this is all right, Miss Lowell," Greer replied. "Now we should begin the search."

Chelsea's rebelliousness deflated. "Of course."

As they passed from room to room with Greer in the lead, Molly was glad Angus seemed willing to be held without protest. She also appreciated the time she and Chelsea had put into cleaning up. At least Chelsea didn't have to wade through the chaotic scene left behind by the burglar who had claimed her uncle's life, whether intentionally or as a by-product of the intrusion. The clean floors and tidy shelves also made it easier to tell that nothing was freshly disturbed.

The cleaning had done nothing to make the house less maze-like though, and Molly still experienced a faint unease every time they went around a corner. Realistically, she felt confident that the intruder was no longer in the building, but it was hard to relax—especially with the image of Myron sprawled on the cold ground so fresh in her mind.

After exploring the downstairs, they headed up the narrow staircase to check the apartment. Chelsea paused at one pile of boxes. "I'm not sure, but I think one of these was moved."

"What do you think?" Greer asked Molly.

Molly winced and cast an apologetic glance toward Chelsea. "I can't tell. It looks untouched to me, but I definitely don't have Chelsea's eye for detail."

Greer used a pen to flip the lid open on the box. "Do the contents appear normal?"

Chelsea and Molly leaned forward to peer into the box, which held a jumble of personal items. "I don't know," Molly said.

"I can't say either." Chelsea sighed. "I think I'm hitting overload."

"I can understand." Greer's tone was gentle. "Let's finish upstairs and go."

The small apartment wasn't exactly tidy, but Molly saw nothing that struck her as different from when she'd been there with Chelsea. She said as much, and Chelsea agreed.

"Okay. It appears that the message is the only definite disturbance," Greer said. "Though there is no way to tell if the note was the intruder's reason for breaking in or if he had other things in mind and Myron Webster interrupted him."

"Greer," Molly said hesitantly. "I don't want to get someone in trouble without cause, but I think you should talk to Sean Mitchum. According to Beverly Scott, he believes his grandmother, Emily Finch, had a valuable collection of jewelry, and no one has been able to find it since her death."

Greer raised an eyebrow. "And you think that could relate to this?"

"The boxes destroyed in this house came from Mrs. Finch's estate," Molly said. "And the message implies the intruder thinks something in this house is his rightful possession. It seems like a fit to me."

"That's sound logic," Greer admitted. "Unfortunately, we are having trouble locating Mitchum. We know he was in Loch Mallaig, and he definitely hasn't gone home. He was staying at the Moose Lake Country Club, but he checked out."

"The country club?" Molly echoed. "But aren't they closed this time of year? I thought even the restaurant was closed in February and March."

"Normally, yes, but apparently Mrs. Finch was an old family friend of the owner. Mr. Mitchum had a room at the country club, but no restaurant access for his time there, then he checked out. We've called all the inns and rooming houses in the area, but no one has a Sean Mitchum registered. He could be using a fake name, I suppose. But I think the search for this man needs to ramp up a little."

"Isn't it hard to register with a fake name these days?" Molly asked. "Besides, the name on the credit card would have to match, and that seems like a lot of hassle. Who would bother?"

"Crooks," Greer answered. "But we'll find him."

"There's one more thing." Molly shifted nervously, knowing the officer wouldn't appreciate what she said next. "Yesterday Chelsea and I found a journal here that belonged to her uncle. I read through it last night, and Ed wrote that someone called the shop and wanted to buy those boxes from the estate, sight unseen, at a healthy profit over what Ed had paid. I think that might have been Sean Mitchum too."

Greer stared at her without speaking for a moment, her face slowly reddening. Molly braced herself for the brewing storm, but Greer's response was quiet—unnervingly quiet. "You found evidence in an active investigation and you're only telling me now?"

"We didn't know it had anything to do with the investigation," Chelsea said defensively. "We didn't want to waste police time if it was unrelated."

"I intended to give it to you all along," Molly said. "Though I have been distracted by Angus's attempted dognapping and Myron Webster's attack."

"Whoa." Greer held up a hand. "Angus was almost dognapped?" She reached out and laid a hand on the little dog's head. "When? Where? Is he okay? He seems okay."

"Last night," Molly said. "I told Michael Drummond about it this morning. I was about to mention the journal to him, but then you came in with the news about Myron, and it flew out of my head." She went on, relating the details of the near dognapping.

"Why would anyone want Angus?" Greer mused aloud. "Aside from his obvious charm, of course."

Molly shook her head. "I have no idea. But I'm keeping him close until I find out."

"Good plan. I can appreciate the potential connection between this break-in and Sean Mitchum, but the dognapping doesn't fit in anywhere."

"Maybe someone thinks Molly knows something," Chelsea said. "And he thought if he had Angus, she'd tell him."

Molly frowned. "But I don't know anything."

"Maybe not, but you do have the journal." Greer gave her a meaningful look. "Which I need you to hand over."

"I don't have it with me," Molly said. "I can drop it by the station, or you can come to Bread on Arrival."

"You'd best take it to the station. Who knows when I'll have a spare minute? And you said you read it?"

"Most of it," Molly said, "and skimmed the rest."

"And the phone call is the only thing that jumped out at you?" Greer pressed.

Molly nodded. "But it doesn't go back all that far. It could be there are more journals. Maybe in one of the unpacked boxes in the apartment."

"We could check," Chelsea suggested.

Greer shook her head. "Not now. This place is a crime scene again, so I'm going to ask you two to go on home and let me work. I'll search the apartment."

Chelsea and Molly carefully exited the back door, taking care not to touch it. Molly immediately put Angus down so he could walk to the car.

"Molly, can I ask a favor?" Chelsea's voice was shaky.

"Of course."

"I know I'm being silly, but that message has me spooked." She laughed, but the sound was brittle. "More spooked than before. Could you follow me to the guesthouse? Once I'm inside, I'll feel better. But I've seen too many scary movies where women are forced off the road."

"No problem. I'll follow you, but once you're inside, I'll need to head to the bakery. I'm shirking my Valentine's Day duties."

"Thank you so much," Chelsea gushed with so much energy that Angus paused in his sniffing to gaze up at her curiously. "I know I'm being a terrible nuisance."

"Not at all," Molly reassured her. "You're far from home and weird things *are* happening. I think you're being completely reasonable."

They walked around the house to the road where the cars were parked. While Chelsea climbed into her car, Molly opened the door of her Honda and Angus hopped in.

"Excuse me?"

Molly spun to see a sixtysomething woman she didn't recognize. "Yes?"

"I'm sorry to bother you." The silver-haired woman pointed up the street. "I live right up there in the blue house. I saw all the cars here and I'm curious. Did something else happen?"

"Myron Webster was found in the backyard."

The woman's eyes widened. "That's why Bernie was barking? I know Mrs. Lordis in the red house heard him. She called me before she called the police to complain." She shook her head. "Mrs. Lordis is scared to death of Bernie. I don't understand it. He's a sweet dog."

"He is," Molly said. She was a little surprised the woman hadn't asked after Myron's well-being. "Do you know Myron well?"

"Is he okay?" the woman asked hesitantly.

"He's alive," Molly said. "And on his way to the hospital."

The woman sighed. "I hate to speak ill of someone who is in the hospital, but yes, I know Myron entirely too well."

"What do you mean?"

"Oh, the man complains about everything. I live next to him. He has the house on the other side of the bookstore. Anyway, I planted a little ornamental tree in my front yard and he was furious. He said it would grow and shade out his plants. Honestly, he patrolled Bernie in front of my yard for months, glaring all the while. Then the bookstore came in and distracted him. I was so glad."

So Myron's glare fests weren't as unusual as Molly had thought.

Chelsea opened her car door. "Molly, is everything okay?"

"Yes," Molly told Chelsea, then turned back to the neighbor. "Sorry, I do need to go."

"No problem," the woman said. "Thanks for letting me know what's going on."

During the drive to the guesthouse, Molly mentally crossed Myron off of her suspect list. He clearly had a history of overreacting to small neighborly slights.

That left Sean Mitchum. She pondered where the man could be hiding. She had thought it unlikely that he'd have friends in Loch Mallaig who would hide him from the police, but she hadn't considered the possibility that he was leaning on his grandmother's friends, as he had with the country club. She didn't envy the police's job of finding a human needle in a large haystack.

When she pulled into a parking spot at the guesthouse, Angus began barking with enthusiasm. "We aren't stopping," she warned him, but his barking only grew more excited.

"You're right," Molly said finally as she shut off the engine. "We should walk Chelsea in, but then we're heading straight to work and you're having some quiet time in the apartment." If Angus had any commentary on that, he kept it to himself.

Molly joined Chelsea near the entrance.

"I didn't mean you had to walk me in," Chelsea said, her cheeks pink.

"It was Angus's idea," Molly said. "He probably thinks Myra will give him a t-r-e-a-t."

"She might," Chelsea agreed as they walked in. "She's so nice."

"I hope you're talking about me," Myra sang out as she walked into the foyer. She peered at Chelsea. "Are you all right, dear? You look a little peaked."

Chelsea put a hand to her cheek. "Do I? It's been quite a day. I'm going to go indulge in a hot bath. I've fallen in love with the claw-foot tub."

Myra beamed at her. "I'm glad. You head right on up and let me know if you need more towels."

"I will." Chelsea flashed a smile at Molly and patted Angus's head. "Thanks again for the escort."

Myra and Molly watched the young woman trot up the stairs. Once she was out of sight, Myra sighed. "I hope the police solve the case soon, before that poor young woman has a breakdown. She's skittish as a cat every night." She shook her head ruefully. "My guests have certainly been through the wringer lately."

"Guests? You have more than one?" She vaguely recalled Myra mentioning that on a previous visit.

"Oh yes, which is a big surprise, as you know. Normally we're lucky to have one guest at a time in February. But I don't envy either of them. One is caught up in this whole mysterious death fiasco, and the other fell down some icy stairs, poor thing."

"Oh no," Molly said. "How awful."

"He told me all about it when I saw him limping this morning. And he can barely work the key in his lock with his bandaged hand. I thought about offering to open the door for him, but you know how men can be sometimes. They hate to admit they need help."

"His hand is bandaged?" Molly asked quietly as warning bells clamored in her mind.

Myra nodded. "He told me he cut it trying to grab for a rusted railing when he fell. Said he had to get a tetanus shot and everything."

"Did he say whose stairs he fell on?" Molly asked.

"No, I didn't think I should ask. There's a fine line between concern and prying."

Molly didn't say anything for a moment as the man's injuries ran through her head. A limp and a bandaged hand. Would the man who'd tried to grab Angus need a bandage? It was possible, even with gloves. Angus had sharp teeth, and he'd been furious at the insult of being grabbed by a stranger. And what if Bernie had gotten in a bite of his own while protecting Myron? Molly imagined that might account for a limp.

Could the man in the guesthouse be Sean Mitchum? Had he been so close this whole time?

14

"Myra," Molly said quietly. "What is the name of your other guest? Is it Sean Mitchum?"

"No, though the police called and asked if we had someone by that name in residence. We didn't. No, the other guest is a history professor, Dr. Richard Hayes."

"A history professor?"

"Yes, he's in Loch Mallaig to do some research on the movement of Scottish immigrants in the United States. I'm sure it's fascinating. Ewan nearly talked his ear off one morning, telling him all about the Loganach family. My husband is so proud of his family heritage."

"And was the professor interested?" Molly asked. If the professor persona was a ruse, it might be hard to maintain interest in a stranger's family history.

"He was . . . polite," Myra said with a giggle. "Ewan does go on sometimes."

"Myra, is the professor kind of thin?" Molly asked, remembering Beverly Scott's description of Sean Mitchum. "In need of a shave?"

Myra's face lit up. "Exactly. I assumed he was the absentminded academic sort. He does have that sort of demeanor. You know what I mean—the kind who forgets to eat and shave when he's deep in his research."

"Actually, Sean Mitchum fits that description."

Myra hooted. "I'm sure a lot of men do. The professor isn't the only untidy man who has ever roomed with us. Thin and scruffy describes Ewan every now and then."

"Of course." Molly still wondered if she should call the police. She had no proof that the man in the guesthouse was Sean Mitchum. He could just as easily be the forgetful professor Myra believed him to be. The bandage could have come from an encounter with Angus or the fall the man had described to Myra. Plus, her little dog certainly hadn't left his dognapper with a limp. It wasn't enough to go on. What she needed was a photo of the supposed professor that she could show to Beverly and find out for sure.

Molly noticed Myra was studying her with an odd expression on her face. "Sorry," she said. "Woolgathering. Is the professor in?"

Myra shook her head. "He left a little while ago, but he did ask about the latest time he could catch a full afternoon tea today. I told him four o'clock. I stretched it a little because he's such a nice man. He assured me he would be back in time for that."

Molly decided that she should be there for that late afternoon tea as well.

After thanking Myra for her time and wishing her a happy Valentine's Day, Molly led a reluctant Angus to the car and drove straight to the bakehouse. The little dog was clearly worn out, but Molly didn't feel completely comfortable leaving him with the run of the apartment. She suspected he was close to reaching the limit of his good behavior when he didn't have free access to the outdoors.

Not wanting to chance mischief once Angus had a refreshing nap, Molly dragged one of his cushions and his beloved stuffed animal, Woolie, into the large storeroom off her apartment. She added a shallow bowl of water and a dog biscuit. Angus happily walked in, flopped down on the cushion with Woolie, and gobbled down his treat. She pulled the door closed behind her and headed for the bakery, but she left the upstairs door open so she could hear if Angus barked. She didn't want him to be miserable, but she would prefer him to be safely contained.

Molly found Laura and Carol far more eager to hear about her morning than to ask her to do any work. "Tell us everything," Carol said as she continued to frost a cake. "We have been climbing the walls while we waited for you."

So Molly related the bits of her morning while Laura and Carol made the appropriate surprised and distressed sounds. When she mentioned Fergus taking Bernie home, Laura and Carol laughed out loud.

"That Fergus has a good heart," Carol said, raising an eyebrow at Molly. "You might do well to remember that."

"I've never doubted that Fergus has a good heart," Molly said. "It's why he's a close friend." She put extra emphasis on "friend," but Carol and Laura only exchanged brief knowing smiles. It was all Molly could do not to growl with exasperation, but she settled for moving on in the story, jumping to the dripping red letters on the mudroom wall.

"That's horrible," Laura said. "Chelsea must be scared half to death."

"All this is getting to her," Molly agreed. "In fact, she asked me to follow her to the guesthouse to make sure she got there all right. But before we left the farmhouse, I learned a few more interesting tidbits." She went on to describe her conversation with Myron's neighbor and the fact that his neighborhood scowl patrol hadn't originated with the opening of the bookstore.

"He sounds like a real piece of work," Laura said.

"But he loves his dog," Carol reminded her. "No one can be all bad if he loves his dog."

Molly was inclined to agree, but she was still glad she didn't have Myron for a neighbor. Finally she related her conversation with Myra. "I'm planning to go back as soon as we close to see if I can get a photo of this professor to show to Beverly."

"As long as you're careful," Carol said. "It would be best if he didn't see you. If it is the same man who tried to grab Angus and hurt Myron, you don't want to give him more reason to target you."

"I don't know why he'd have any reason in the first place, but hopefully the police can ask him about that, if it does turn out to be Sean Mitchum."

Laura paused in her task of painting bread pans with butter. "Well, whatever you do, I don't think you should do it alone. If this is a dangerous person, you shouldn't face him by yourself."

"I have no intention of facing him at all," Molly assured her. "I intend to hide and take a picture."

"Still, having someone along could prove helpful if things go wrong," Laura said. "You should take Hamish. He's working today. I know he won't mind if it will help keep you safe."

Molly considered the idea. She was fond of Hamish despite his gruff, curmudgeonly demeanor. And he was a good person to have in a tight situation since there weren't many people Hamish couldn't intimidate. But when she tried to imagine hiding for who knows how long with Hamish grumbling in her ear about whatever bee he had in his bonnet this week, she quickly discarded the idea of bringing him.

"I could ask Fergus," she said hesitantly as a pang of guilt cut through her. She was fairly sure Fergus would agree, but he'd already been pulled away from work because of his concern for her. And on top of that, he now had a very large houseguest.

"That's an excellent idea," Carol said.

"It would be more pleasant," Laura added with a wide grin.

Molly ignored the implied teasing and said, "Good. I'll call him now, and then I'm going to work. I've played enough hooky for one day."

Fergus immediately agreed to meet her at the guesthouse after the bakery closed. "I love a good spy mission."

"You're sure it won't be a problem?" Molly asked. "I have kept you away from work a lot."

"That's one of the best things about having a great staff and a brilliant son," he said. "They pretty much handle everything. I just got here actually, and they show no sign of having missed me at all."

"You sound oddly cheerful about being replaceable," Molly said.

"I know I'd be missed eventually, and the proud dad in me loves seeing Neil excel."

"How's Bernie settling in at your house?" Molly asked.

"Quite nicely. We went for a romp along the shore, then I left him napping. I told Neil about him, and it was all I could do to keep him from driving directly to the house to play with the dog. It's enough to make me feel guilty for not getting him more pets as a kid."

"I'm glad to hear you're still happy with your new roommate."

"I don't know how happy my house cleaner will be. As far as I can tell, Bernie's main hobbies are shedding hair and drooling."

Molly winced, but she was glad she hadn't brought the dog to the apartment. At least Fergus had a house cleaner. She finalized a time to meet Fergus at the guesthouse and hung up. Then she made a call to Myra. "I have a quick favor to ask of you," she said.

"Anything," Myra said cheerfully.

"If your professor comes to tea before I get there, would you please call me? I want to get a look at the man."

"Sure, no problem," Myra said. "But I'm absolutely certain that he is not involved with any crimes."

Molly couldn't even say that she hoped Myra was right, considering she felt the opposite. She actually hoped to have found the man who had committed burglary, assault, and possibly murder. But she did thank the innkeeper again before hanging up. Shoving the phone in her pocket, Molly smiled at her friends. "I'm all yours now."

Before either Laura or Carol could respond, they were interrupted by a high-pitched scream.

15

Molly, Laura, and Carol rushed to the front of the bakehouse, where a broad-shouldered woman pointed toward the fireplace. To Molly's shock, Angus sat on the stone hearth, staring at the woman with obvious disdain.

"Angus!" Molly scolded. "How did you get down here?" She grabbed the little dog and turned to the woman. "What happened?"

"That animal accosted me," the woman insisted.

"Angus is barely eye level with a grasshopper," Hamish said. "How could such a wee critter accost you?"

"I came over here to warm myself by the fire," the woman said. "I saw the creature, of course, but I assumed he wasn't real. After all, who would have a real dog in an eating establishment?"

"He isn't supposed to be here," Molly assured her. "He must have snuck downstairs."

"Well, I should hope he isn't supposed to be here," the woman said, her tone still stiff. "At any rate, the creature put his cold nose against my leg, right above the edge of my boot. He scared me half to death."

"That's hardly a capital offense," Hamish grumbled.

"We are sorry," Laura said after giving Hamish a quelling glance. Laura was one of the few who could offer Hamish a look stern enough to hush him up, at least for a moment. "Why don't you pick out a pastry and have a cup of coffee? On us, of course."

The woman pulled her coat tighter around her, but she seemed to be calming slightly. "I suppose." She gave Angus one last glare. "I wouldn't have gone anywhere near the beast if I'd known it was real."

"Of course not," Laura said, her voice soothing. "Come with me and we'll find you something you'd enjoy."

As the women moved away, Molly frowned at Angus. "How did you get downstairs?"

Carol patted her arm. "Don't worry about it. A little excitement is good for people." She grinned. "That customer can claim it as her cardio for the day."

Hamish chuckled, then held out his hands. "Why don't you let me give Angus a run around the block? Then maybe he'll be too tired for mischief."

"I thought he would have been too tired for mischief already." Molly handed over the dog. "There's a leash hanging near the back door. I'm going to run up and see if I can tell how he got out."

When she got upstairs, she saw that the storage room door was open. She walked inside and closed the door, then pushed on it. The door swung open easily. "Good job, Molly." She shook her head at her own oversight. She'd never tried closing Angus in the storage room before, so she hadn't known about the faulty door.

With a sigh, she dragged the dog's belongings out of the room and shut the door behind her. She'd have to let him have the run of the apartment after all and trust that he'd behave.

"Hopefully I'll identify Sean Mitchum this afternoon," she said aloud. "And then all of this will be over."

Molly threw herself into work when she got downstairs, hoping to make up for her morning. She helped Bridget run the front until Hamish returned, then she went back to the kitchen to pack up the day's shipments and bag fresh rolls for a local restaurant. She finished by working on an Easter promotional campaign she had in mind. By closing time, Molly had expunged most of her guilt.

As they washed pans together at the kitchen sink, Carol said, "Molly, why don't I take Angus home with me for the afternoon? He'll love a chance to play with Pascal." Carol's gray-and-white cat was the definition of shy, as he spent most of his time out of sight.

Molly laughed, amazed that Carol had made the suggestion with a straight face. "Pascal hates Angus. You and I both know it. He hides under the bed whenever we come over."

"He hides under the bed no matter what," Carol argued. "Even if Pascal wouldn't be thrilled, Harvey would be. He adores Angus."

It would mean I wouldn't have to worry about Angus while I'm away . . . Molly finally agreed. "Hopefully it'll be only this once, and I'll be setting the police on the man by evening."

When Molly reached Two Scots Guesthouse, she found Fergus already there, chatting on his phone in his car. She waited for him to finish the call, then waved. He hopped out. "I didn't see you, sorry," he said. "You should have rapped on the window."

"I didn't mind waiting."

Fergus hunched in his coat. "I thought women were supposed to be cold all the time."

Molly laughed. "It comes and goes." She headed for the door with Fergus beside her. "I figure my phone should take a good enough photo to do the job, and I can send it straight to Beverly, then to Greer if Beverly identifies this man as Sean Mitchum."

"Sounds like a plan." Fergus opened the door for Molly. "Are we going to wait at a table in the dining room?"

"No, I'd rather he didn't see me. I thought we could stake out the situation from the kitchen."

They headed down a short hall to a door that led directly to the kitchen, bypassing the dining room in case their target was already there. In the cheerful, brightly-lit kitchen, Myra was pouring water into a china teapot decorated with delicate paintings of thistles. Her face lit as she recognized them. "Good afternoon, Fergus," she said. "I knew Molly was coming, but it's nice to see you."

"Always good to see you," Fergus replied. "How's Ewan?"

"He's great," Myra said. "He's upstairs working on a dripping sink. It's always something around here, but I suppose it's good to stay busy."

Fergus nodded. "I know how that is."

"The professor isn't here yet," Myra said, answering Molly's unasked question. "But he should be here soon. He promised that I wouldn't have to hold tea for him. Do you two want to grab a table?"

"No, I thought we would wait in here and watch through the doorway to the dining room if it's all right with you," Molly said. "I'd rather the man didn't see me, but I need a photo of him to show someone who can say absolutely whether it's Sean Mitchum."

Myra sniffed. "I'm sure it's not, but you don't want to wait in here. My guests often come in the kitchen to chat, including the professor."

"Do you have a suggestion?" Fergus asked.

Myra took a moment to contemplate, then grinned. "I do know somewhere. You may not enjoy it."

"If it will work as a hiding spot, I'll love it," Molly assured her, refusing to acknowledge the unease she felt at Myra's grin.

Myra led them into the dining room, where two women Molly recognized from church sat sipping tea and nibbling on biscuits and cheese. The women waved at Molly and Fergus. For a moment, Molly expected to wait for Fergus to stop and chat, but he merely waved back. She appreciated him prioritizing their mission.

Myra crossed the dining room and opened a pair of double doors that led to a completely empty closet. "I'm planning to have Ewan take the doors off this closet and repaint the inside so I can use it as a serving alcove. But for now, it should work for your purpose. Once you close the door, the professor will never see you. You can watch through the crack between the doors."

The closet offered enough space for two people, but not a lot more. Molly knew it was going to be tight quarters for her and Fergus, especially if they tried to peer out the crack between the doors at the same time—but if it let her get the photo, she'd do it. She risked a glance toward the women at the table and noticed them watching with great interest. *Terrific. The gossip from this experience should be interesting.*

"I think this will do perfectly," Fergus said as he stepped into the closet.

"I still think it's silly," Myra said. "You're going to find out that Professor Hayes is a history scholar and nothing more."

"You could be right." Molly took a deep breath, casting aside concerns for the gossip she was getting ready to fuel, and stepped into the closet. Fergus pulled the doors almost closed.

"Okay," Myra said from outside. "I'll see you both whenever." She spun and headed to the kitchen.

With the door closed, Molly was even more aware of the closeness of the space in the shadowy closet. She was grateful that she'd never suffered from claustrophobia.

"This is nostalgic," Fergus whispered close to her ear, his breath tickling the side of her face.

"Nostalgic?" Molly asked as she eased away slightly, only to feel her elbow connect with the closet wall.

"Don't you remember that time we were accidentally locked in the housekeeper's supply room at the resort? You were helping me do some chores for my dad."

"And you managed to get us locked in the closet by horsing around. As I remember, you were recreating some moment in a horror movie," Molly said. "I was so angry with you for that little trick."

"As I remember, you were annoyed with me a lot."

"Because you were a terrible tease," Molly said defensively. "And you gave me nightmares with your constant stories from scary movies."

"I didn't get to see all those movies," he admitted. "Sometimes I was working from trailers, but I think I dabbled with the idea of being a movie director around that time, which was part of my interest."

"I had no idea you wanted to be a movie director."

"Most kids do, don't they? Either that or a famous rock star. For me, the movie director phase was sandwiched between astronaut and business executive."

"And you went with business executive," Molly said.

"It seemed better suited to my skills. I have no idea how to begin directing a movie."

Molly realized that the whispered chatting had helped ease her discomfort about the tight space in the closet. She leaned close to the crack in the door, but she only saw the two church ladies. At least they'd lost interest in staring at the closet doors.

"As I think about it," Fergus said. "There's something else I remember about being locked in that supply room closet."

Molly straightened to stare at Fergus. She could barely make out his features by the dim light in the closet. "What's that?"

"I remember thinking about how beautiful you were when you were so mad at me."

A blush crept up Molly's cheeks. "You like angry women? Dating you must be a treat." Then she felt even more embarrassed about bringing up dating. Hopefully he wouldn't think she was hinting, which she was not.

"I try to assume dating me is a positive experience, not that I have a lot of folks to testify to that," he admitted. "But I definitely liked *you* back then, Molly."

Molly didn't know what to say, so she said nothing.

"You were so much fun," he went on in his hushed tone. "You thought a lot of my ideas were silly, but you always came along. I think I spent every summer trying to amuse you. I loved the sound of your laugh."

"I had no idea," she said softly.

"And that was what I liked best."

Molly was struck speechless again as Fergus leaned closer to her. He rested a hand gently on her upper arm before he kissed her. And to her absolute surprise, she found herself kissing him back.

16

Like a splash of cold water, Molly suddenly realized exactly what she was doing, hiding in a closet, kissing one of her oldest friends. She jumped back as much as the tight confines would allow, which wasn't much, and held up both hands.

"Molly?" Fergus murmured, but she couldn't face him.

What have I done? Surely she'd ruined their friendship, a friendship she valued almost above any other. *Okay, he kissed me first,* she reasoned with herself, *but I definitely kissed him back.*

"Molly, are you all right?" Fergus asked again, his voice full of concern.

To cover her flustered emotions, she gestured toward the door. "I think something's happening," she lied and focused her own attention on the room beyond the closet.

To her utter shock, she found she hadn't been lying after all. Myra was talking to a rather rumpled man with a bandaged hand. Molly blinked. The man was distinctly familiar. Perhaps she'd seen him at the bakehouse. It had felt as if all of Loch Mallaig had filed through in the last few days. The man didn't radiate menace. No one would suspect him of being a killer or a burglar. But Molly had more reason than most to know that the bad guys rarely wore signs identifying themselves.

"That's him," she whispered to Fergus.

She slipped her phone from her pocket and began snapping photos through the crack between doors. She took as many as she could. Most were in profile as he talked to Myra, but then Molly had a heart-stopping moment when the man shrugged out of his coat and started toward the closet. Myra caught his arm and said something to him before taking his coat herself and walking over to the corner where an antique coat rack stood. Despite her burst of anxiety, Molly caught several photos of the man's full face.

Once she was certain she had more than enough photos for an identification, she quickly texted the photos to Beverly. Then, with a sigh of relief, she slipped her phone into her pocket and peered at Fergus's slightly shadowed face. Of course, the kiss was still hanging in the air between them. Molly cast one longing look toward the closet doors, but she could hardly run out into the dining room while the man was eating. She was stuck in the closet with Fergus and the ghost of the kiss.

"Molly," Fergus whispered. "I'm sorry. I guess I got caught up in the holiday and the nostalgia. I shouldn't have taken advantage."

Even in the poor lighting, Molly could see the remorse on Fergus's face. "You didn't take advantage," she said. "I didn't exactly fight you off. It was nostalgia, like you said. And probably the insanity that comes with being unattached on Valentine's Day." As the words tumbled out of her mouth, she felt her cheeks warm with embarrassment. For once she was grateful for the poor lighting in the closet.

"Still, it wasn't fair," Fergus said. "And I will kick myself forever if it hurts our friendship in any way."

"No," Molly said, her volume raising slightly at the shock of what he'd said. She quickly put a hand over her mouth and then whispered again. "There's no reason for this to hurt our friendship. We can chalk it up to the heat of the moment and forget it." *As if I could ever forget it.*

"Whatever will keep our friendship intact," Fergus assured her.

"Good. And maybe it would be best if we didn't talk about it," Molly said. "Or tell anyone."

Fergus smiled. "Even if it hadn't been an aberration, I'm not a guy who kisses and tells."

Again Molly's cheeks felt as if they might ignite at any moment. "Good. I'm glad we can put this behind us."

"Of course."

Molly peeked through the crack in the door again and saw that Myra was bringing out a pot of tea and a plate of pastries and cheese for the rumpled man. *Eat fast, please.*

To Molly's immense relief, the man she believed to be Sean Mitchum didn't linger over his tea and treats. When he finally left the dining room, Molly practically burst through the closet doors, grateful that the church ladies had finished their own tea long before and she didn't have to worry about an audience noting how embarrassed she still felt. She could hardly believe how good the fresher air felt on her flushed cheeks.

Standing in the empty dining room, Molly pulled out her phone, hoping for a response from Beverly, but none had arrived. "I'm going to drive over to Lochside Realty," she told Fergus. "Beverly hasn't answered my text, and I want to know if she recognizes our erstwhile professor."

"Do you want me to come with you?" Fergus asked.

Molly definitely did not. She needed a little time away from Fergus to sort out the emotional jumble inside her. "No, but thank you. You should probably get to Castleglen before your son forgets you run the place."

Fergus laughed. "Now that could actually be a possibility. Okay, call if you need me. And don't do anything dangerous by yourself."

"I don't plan to do anything dangerous at all," Molly assured him.

She popped into the kitchen to thank Myra for helping out with their clandestine photography. The other woman frowned, but said, "I helped because I know the professor will be proven innocent. He's a nice man. You'll see."

"You could be right," Molly agreed pleasantly. She didn't think Myra was right at all, but anything was possible. It seemed to be a day when the absolute craziest thing could happen.

When Molly reached Lochside Realty, she found Beverly at the door, ready to walk in. "Beverly," Molly called. "Wait."

Beverly turned, recognized Molly, and waved. "Hi. Let me guess—you're finally ready to find a house instead of living over the bakery."

"No," Molly said. "I love my little apartment. I came by to hear what you thought of the photos I sent."

"Photos?"

"I texted them a while ago."

Beverly pulled her phone from her purse, then frowned at the screen when it wouldn't power on. "Oh rats. I forgot to charge it. Honestly, I've been a little discombobulated since the break-in. You'd best come on inside where it's warm and show me the photos. Do you have them with you?"

"On my phone." Molly followed Beverly into the warm reception area and through to the office beyond. As she walked, she dug out her phone from her purse.

"Hold on a second." Beverly fished in one of the desk drawers and pulled out a charger. She plugged it into the wall, then hooked up her phone while Molly fidgeted. "Okay, all set. Show me the pictures."

Molly held up the phone displaying the clearest photo she had of the alleged professor.

Beverly took one look and nodded. "That's definitely Sean Mitchum."

"I knew it." Molly flipped her phone around to view the screen. "I need to call the police station and let them know where they can find him."

"Good," Beverly said firmly. "If he's the one who broke in here, I hope they throw the book at him. I could hardly sleep last night for the nerves."

Molly called Greer right away. Her friend answered with a chipper, "Molly! What catastrophe do you have for me now?"

"No catastrophe at all," Molly said. "But I found Sean Mitchum. He's staying at Two Scots Guesthouse under the name Richard Hayes. I took a photo of him, and Beverly Scott has identified him as Sean Mitchum."

"Can you send me the photo?" Greer asked.

"Hold on. I'll text it to you." Molly quickly sent the photo. "Okay, it's on the way."

Greer didn't answer for a moment, then said, "Got it. This is a weird angle. Where were you?"

Molly backed away from Beverly's desk and answered softly. "The closet in the dining room."

Greer hooted with laughter. "Molly Ferris, you're a never-ending surprise. You do know you could have told me you thought the guy was Mitchum. I'd have checked him out."

"You have enough on your plate. I wanted to be sure."

"I suppose I appreciate that, but I do wish you'd be careful. We'd hate to lose you on The Piping Yoopers."

"Only because my playing makes the rest of you sound better by comparison. Can you tell me how Myron Webster is doing?"

"Actually, I received a call from the hospital right before you called. He has regained consciousness, though he's still not out of the woods. Michael and I will be going over to question him, but not until after we pick up Mitchum. If Mitchum did attack Mr. Webster, I'm sure it'll be a relief to know the man is in custody."

"I'm sure it will be," Molly agreed. She also thought it would be a relief for Myron to hear that Bernie was well and in a safe place. In fact, Molly decided to drive over to the hospital and see if they'd let her visit Myron. She could see for herself how he was doing.

Her musings made her miss something Greer said, and she had to ask the officer to repeat it. "I said I hope when we search Mitchum's room, we find the can of paint used to vandalize the bookstore."

"That would be helpful," Molly said. "I'll leave you to it. Take care."

"I could say the same to you, but you never listen."

As Molly ended the call, she noticed that Beverly had slipped a little closer to eavesdrop. The real estate agent smiled apologetically, clearly mildly embarrassed. "Sorry, I shouldn't have been listening, but I've been a mess since the break-in. I wanted to think it was over."

"I believe it will be soon," Molly assured her, understanding completely. "The police will be picking him up right away, and I'm sure they'll find some kind of evidence in his room at the guesthouse. And they'll owe a lot of that to you. Thanks for identifying him."

"I'm glad to be of help." Beverly smoothed her skirt. "I will breathe much easier when he's in custody. Do you suppose the police will let me know when that happens?"

"I hope so," Molly said. "I could use the reassurance myself."

"Say, would you like a cup of coffee? I know I need one if I'm going to get through the rest of the day without a nap. You wouldn't believe how long it took me to cover up the effects of poor sleep last night." She patted her cheek, which was perfectly made up as always. Molly wished she was as good at hiding sleeplessness.

"You look great. Thanks again for your help and the offer of coffee, but I need to head out. Oh, and happy Valentine's Day."

Beverly smiled. "You too."

When Molly was settled in her car, she quickly made a few calls to catch everyone up on the identification of Sean Mitchum. She began with Laura, keeping details brief and leaving out any mention of kisses in the closet.

"I'm glad to hear the police are picking him up," Laura said. "I've been worried about you."

"I've been worried about me too," Molly admitted. "I hope you have a nice Valentine's Day evening."

Laura snorted. "I'm spending it in the best possible way—alone with a good book."

Carol answered the phone for the next call and Molly quickly told her that she'd found Sean Mitchum. "He's staying at Two Scots Guesthouse. The police are on the way to pick him up."

"He's been in the same guesthouse as Chelsea this whole time," Carol said, shocked. "I hope she's okay."

Molly realized she hadn't thought of that. Did that put the young woman in danger? "I should call Chelsea and let her know."

"Don't worry about that," Carol said. "I'll grab Harvey and Angus and head over there right now. We can bring the poor girl here and keep her safe until the police have that ruffian in hand."

"That's an excellent idea."

"Are you on your way to your apartment?" Carol asked.

"Not yet. I thought I'd go to the hospital and check on Myron Webster. Greer said he's regained consciousness, and I wanted to let him know that Bernie is safe and happy with Fergus."

"Is Fergus still with you?" Carol asked, and Molly was glad the other woman couldn't see her as a flush spread up her cheeks at the question.

I've got to get a grip on myself. "No, he went back to work."

"Oh, maybe after you visit the hospital, you should come here too," Carol said. "At least until the police pick up that awful man."

"I'm sure I'll be fine, but I will be by to get Angus after I'm done at the hospital. I shouldn't be long. I don't even know if the hospital will let me see Myron."

"You take as long as you need," Carol said. "Angus will be good therapy for Chelsea. I doubt Pascal will avail himself for comfort cuddles."

"You're probably right about that," Molly said with a chuckle. "See you soon." She was glad her friends would be with Chelsea. The girl needed a feeling of family around her—and to be as far away from Sean Mitchum as possible.

17

Prodded by a cold breeze, Molly strode into the hospital as quickly as she dared, considering the potential for black ice in the parking lot. She stopped at the information desk and asked for Myron Webster's room number.

The elderly woman at the desk smiled brightly at her. "You're in luck," she said. "It looks like they've just cleared him for visitors."

Relief washed over Molly. If they were allowing guests, Myron must be doing better. She thanked the woman for her help and took the visitor's badge, sticking it to the lapel of her coat. As she walked toward the ward, she passed the gift shop and detoured inside, intending to buy some flowers. To her surprise, she found Fergus standing in front of the cooler, running his hand through his thick, dark hair as he pondered the selection.

"Fergus!" Her immediate pleasure at seeing him quickly grew awkward, and her cheeks warmed.

"I assume great minds think alike," he said. "You're here to see Myron too? I wanted to let him know that Bernie was in good hands."

"I had the same thought, and to tell him the man who attacked him is hopefully in police custody by now," Molly said. "I know I would worry about that if I were in here."

"Then we can visit together." He pointed at the cooler. "Want to split a bouquet? There's only so much space for these things in those tiny hospital rooms, and I'm open to suggestions about which one to pick."

"That sounds good." Molly could feel the awkwardness between them draining away. Sure, they'd kissed, but they were still friends. They could put that one moment behind them.

She helped Fergus pick out a nice arrangement and insisted on paying her fair share, though Fergus protested that she could pay him later.

"If I do it now, I don't have to remember later," Molly said as she handed him the money. She heard him mutter something that might have been "stubborn," but she chose to ignore it.

A few minutes later, a stern nurse coming out of Myron's room blocked their approach. "No guests allowed."

"I was told at the front desk that Mr. Webster could have visitors," Molly said.

"You were told wrong. He needs his rest." The nurse eyed the flowers as if they were a wilted mass of weeds instead of a cheery bouquet of daisies and roses. "I can take those."

"Nurse Matthews," Fergus said reasonably, reading from the woman's name tag. "I can understand Myron's need for rest, but he also needs freedom from worry. I know he's concerned about his dog, and I want to tell him the dog is safe and sound with me."

The woman crossed her arms. "He hasn't mentioned a dog."

"But he can talk?" Molly asked.

The nurse's frown deepened, but she nodded. "He can. And he is worried about a family member. Someone named Bernie. I assume it's his child? If you know that Bernie is well, I'll be glad to tell Mr. Webster that."

"Bernie is his dog," Fergus said. "And I don't mean to argue, truly, but Myron isn't going to simply take your word for it. I can show him photos of Bernie, happy and well cared for." He brought his phone out of his pocket and tapped on the screen a few times. He held up a photo of the massive dog inside Fergus's house, sprawled on the well-polished floor near the huge bank of dining room windows that showed the icy loch beyond.

The nurse stared at the phone without speaking for a long moment. Then her expression softened. "All right," she said. "You can go in since an *extremely short* visit could relieve the patient's anxiety. But no more than five minutes, and I *will* be timing you."

Molly and Fergus didn't give the woman a chance to change her mind. They darted around her and into Myron's room.

They found him propped up in bed, his face reflecting surprise at their sudden appearance. "Molly?"

"Hello, Myron," Molly said. "I'm so glad to hear you're feeling better. This is my friend, Fergus MacGregor."

Myron blinked at him. "Oh yes, I remember you now. I met you on the street with Molly."

"That's right." Fergus held up the floral arrangement. "We brought you some flowers and some good news. Bernie is safe. He's staying at my house, and he's already found his favorite spot by the windows where he can see the loch."

Myron smiled, an expression that transformed his pale face. "Really? I was so worried he was in the dog pound or running loose. Thank you for coming to tell me."

"I can even show you." Fergus handed Myron his phone with the photo of Bernie. "He'll be happy and healthy whenever you get home and are ready to have him back."

Myron stared at it for a long moment. A single tear ran down his face. Myron wiped it away and handed Fergus his phone. "Thank you again. You don't know how worried I've been."

"I could guess," Molly assured him. "I'd feel the same way about Angus. Myron, could you tell us what happened? How did you end up behind the bookstore?"

"I was walking Bernie as usual," Myron explained. "We often go by the front of the bookstore since walking in the other direction puts us next to Mrs. Dunwoody's house. She frets that Bernie is going to give her cats a heart attack if they spot him through the windows, though I don't know how her cats could possibly see Bernie with the massive tree she planted in her front yard. Anyway, we'd nearly passed the bookstore when Bernie suddenly dragged me behind the house. Bernie is a good dog, but when he wants to go somewhere, he puts a lot of muscle behind it."

"I can imagine," Molly agreed, picturing the giant canine. "Did you see something behind the house?"

Myron nodded. "A man in several layers of clothing was tinkering with the back door. My dog is normally a gentle soul, but he didn't react well to that man at all. He snarled at him."

"Good judge of character," Fergus said.

"He usually is." Myron smiled proudly. "I yelled at the man, asking him what he was doing. I suppose the guy must have panicked, because he threw something at me. I couldn't even tell you what. I vaguely remember it hitting my head and that's about it. The next thing I knew, I was in this bed, panicking about my dog."

Molly took out her phone and brought up the photo of Sean Mitchum. "Could this be the man who attacked you?"

Myron studied the photo, then shrugged. "Maybe? I didn't see the man clearly. I thought he was heavier than that, but it may have been the winter clothes. I do think the man who attacked me had a beard . . . maybe."

Disappointment washed over Molly. She had hoped Myron could offer an identification. She started to ask another question, but the nurse bustled in and announced, "Enough. Surely you've told him about the dog, and now Mr. Webster needs to rest. Out with you both."

"Thank you for coming," Myron said as the nurse stepped between his visitors and the bed.

"One moment." Fergus pulled a business card from his wallet. "Here's my phone number. You can call or text me anytime for an update on Bernie. I promise he'll be treated well."

The nurse relented enough to allow Fergus to pass the card to Myron, who said, "I only hope he'll want to come home after staying in such a beautiful place."

"I wouldn't worry about that." Molly smiled warmly. "Bernie clearly loves you very much. He wouldn't let anyone near you until Angus and I showed up. I think Angus convinced him everything would be okay."

"Bless you both," Myron said hoarsely.

This marked the end of the nurse's patience, and she shooed Molly and Fergus out into the hall before returning to her patient. Molly heard her ask him about his regular medications and she paused to listen.

Myron named two medications Molly was unfamiliar with, but he helpfully explained that both prescriptions were for his blood pressure. "I also take something to stave off the symptoms from those meds," he said. "Isn't that the way medication works sometimes? The cure is often worse than the disease."

Molly felt a little guilty eavesdropping outside a hospital room. She started down the hall to meet Fergus, who had already moved away and then stopped to wait for her.

"Hear anything interesting?" he teased as they walked toward the exit.

Molly sensed a blush creeping in and wondered if she should get used to being perpetually red-faced now. "I feel guilty enough already, but no. Nothing special. I should go pick up Angus from Carol's house and head home. I can put in some time working in the office to make me feel better about being away so much while the bakehouse was open."

When they reached the parking lot, Fergus walked her to her car and then said, "I'm going to run by the house and check on Bernie, then head to work myself. But let me know if you need me for anything."

"I doubt you'll hear from me tonight," Molly told him. "I'm planning a quiet evening at home with Angus."

"If this is the last I see you today, happy Valentine's Day," Fergus said. His tone was light, but Molly knew he must be thinking about earlier in the closet.

"Y-you too," she stammered, suddenly quite nervous. She swiftly climbed in her Honda and drove off with a wave.

When she got to Carol's house to pick up Angus, she found Chelsea wasn't there. "We tried to talk her into coming," Carol explained, "but she said she was tired of being scared. The Loganachs promised to watch over her, so we let it go. Now, tell me all about your visit with Myron."

"Sure," Molly agreed. "Though it wasn't particularly eventful." As soon as Molly mentioned running into Fergus, however, it was clear Carol considered *that* eventful.

"He wanted to reassure Myron that his dog was well cared for." Molly tried to keep her voice light, but Carol peered at her closely and Molly knew her friend suspected there was something Molly wasn't saying. The memory of what she was hiding made her cheeks warm and she couldn't miss the knowing glance that passed between Harvey and Carol.

"If you're going to tease me," Molly said to head off any possible comment, "I'll take my dog and go. We've had a long day."

"Nothing was further from my mind," Carol assured her before patting her husband's arm. "You're probably going to have to go fetch Angus. Last I saw him, he was napping under the bed in the cat's spot while Pascal glared at him and plotted revenge in his little kitty heart."

"Poor Pascal," Harvey said with a laugh. "I'll go get Angus. I'm sure he'll appreciate a friendly face."

As Harvey left the room, Carol examined Molly. Instead of bringing up Fergus, however, she asked, "So Myron didn't offer anything useful?"

Molly shook her head. "He couldn't identify who had attacked him, but I feel sure it was Sean Mitchum. I don't suppose you've gotten any calls about the man being captured, have you? Not even from the Loch Mallaig gossip network?"

"Nope. All calls to the house since I talked to you have been from my grandchildren."

As if the very discussion was an omen, Molly's phone rang. When she checked the screen, her eyes widened. "Police," she told Carol before connecting the call. "Hello, this is Molly Ferris."

"And this is Officer Drummond," the male voice said. "I wanted to let you know that we haven't been able to find Sean Mitchum. He hasn't been back to Two Scots Guesthouse. We're searching for him, but he is still at large. You need to be careful, Molly. I would recommend staying with a friend tonight instead of being alone in the bakehouse."

"I'll give that some thought," Molly said, then thanked him for calling and hung up.

"You've gone pale," Carol said. "Do you need to sit?"

Molly forced a tight smile. "No, I'm all right. Officer Drummond wanted to let me know they haven't found Sean Mitchum yet. He said I should be careful."

"That's it." Carol wagged a finger at Molly. "You and Angus should stay with us tonight. You'll be safe as houses here."

"I think I've taken advantage of you and Harvey enough for one day," Molly said.

Carol huffed derisively. "Not even in the slightest. You know you're both welcome here. Harvey loves you as much as I do."

Molly knew Harvey wouldn't mind if she stayed, but she loathed the idea of being run out of her home. Plus, there was no reason to believe Sean Mitchum would be coming to the bakehouse. She was fairly certain he'd already been there.

"Angus and I will be going home," Molly said firmly. "I appreciate the offer so much, but we'll be perfectly safe."

Though Carol tried more coaxing, even offering to call Laura for a slumber party at the bakehouse, Molly finally managed to convince her that she'd take all reasonable precautions.

About the time Carol gave up arguing, Harvey came back with Angus in tow. The little dog greeted Molly with wild enthusiasm, making her laugh. "You'd think he hadn't seen me in days."

"If you believe in dog years, it probably felt like days," Harvey said. "But I know he had a good time. I can't say the same for Pascal."

Carol chuckled. "I expect with a few extra treats, Pascal will forget the trauma of having a lovable Scottie in the house for a few hours soon enough."

Molly listened with affection as Carol and Harvey discussed their plans for dinner and was especially glad she hadn't agreed to stay. She didn't want to be a third wheel on Valentine's Day.

"You know," Carol said slyly, "it's a little late to start something. I suppose we'll simply have leftovers. I think I have some kale for salad."

Harvey groaned. "I can take a hint. We can dine out, as long as we don't call it a Valentine's Day dinner. I don't need a holiday to remind me to treat my wife like a queen."

"That's true enough," Carol said fondly.

"I'll leave you two to decide what to do for your non-holiday dinner," Molly said. "Thank you both again for keeping Angus for the afternoon." She gave Carol an impulsive hug and whispered in her ear, "Happy Valentine's Day."

"You too."

With the cheerful sound of her friends still in her head, Molly and Angus headed out into the cold. Molly shivered as the chill seeped through her, and she hurried to the car. Angus must not have enjoyed the cold either because he didn't try to linger, not even to sniff in the direction of the chicken coop. Once Molly had Angus settled, she quickly started the car to get the heater going. She didn't immediately drive away, though. She had to admit, it did seem a little bit sad to be home alone on Valentine's Day.

"I'm being silly," she told Angus. "After all, I get to spend Valentine's Day with my best guy."

Angus yipped in agreement.

When they drew near Bread on Arrival, Molly decided to take Angus for a quick walk around the park before the night settled in full force. She drove past the bakehouse and pulled into one of the small parking areas at Dumfries Park. Streetlamps along the path showed a few other dog walkers, and knowing that she and Angus wouldn't be alone on their walk made her feel safer.

Greeting other pet owners along the way helped keep Molly from watching the shadows fretfully. She would be glad when the police finally announced the capture of Sean Mitchum. She had no intention of giving in to her fear, but that didn't mean she wasn't aware of it.

When she and Angus were finally snug and warm in the bakehouse again, Molly took a moment to check all the locks downstairs and collect a loaf of bread from the day-old rack. A few toasted slices would go well with soup for supper, which seemed the perfect cure for the cold that had crept into her bones during the walk. As she passed through the downstairs rooms, she realized how tired she was. The last few days were finally catching up with her.

If Angus felt the same, he showed no sign. In fact, he zoomed in and out of each room in the apartment as soon as they got upstairs, skidding around the corners as he went.

Watching Angus's wild race helped Molly shake off some of her weariness as she laughed heartily each time he darted into the kitchen to gaze up at her, panting blithely, then dashed off again.

"I thought trying to get Carol's poor cat to play with you would have worn you out," she told him during one of his brief pauses.

The next time he slid into the kitchen, Molly was pouring soup into a bowl. Angus raced around her for a few laps before heading out the door again. For some reason she thought of the woman who'd been frightened by Angus downstairs, mistaking him for a fake dog because he was asleep. "No one could mistake him for a stuffed dog tonight."

Then it hit her. The woman had thought Angus was a fake dog. He'd been sleeping exactly as he had been in her arms when Sean Mitchum tried to grab him. And in that instant, she knew exactly why Mitchum wanted to pry a dog from her grasp.

Molly set the soup pot in the sink and hurried to the closet where she'd stored and completely forgotten the Scottie dog statue she'd bought at the bookstore. She flipped the statue upside down. Someone had hastily patched the bottom of the figure. The patch felt different from the surrounding ceramic material, rougher but very hard.

Molly held the dog close to her ear and shook it, listening for anything moving inside. She thought she heard a faint rustling. Angus rushed up to her and, upon seeing the detested statue, promptly barked at it.

"Hush, Angus. There's more to this dog than meets the eye." She carried the ceramic dog into the kitchen and pulled a sturdy knife from the drawer. She spent some time trying to pry the patch away. She was almost ready to give up when the plug finally popped out.

Molly shook the statue a few times, and an irregular bundle wrapped in a paper napkin fell from the hole. As soon as the bundle struck the counter, the napkin tore and glittering jewelry poured out. An ornate necklace with impressively large rubies, emeralds, and diamonds was joined by matching earrings, a diamond tennis bracelet, and a strand of lustrous pearls.

She was still staring at the mound of jewels when Angus began barking furiously again. Molly turned to scold him for yapping at the statue, but Angus wasn't in the doorway to the kitchen. Molly left the statue on the counter and went looking for her dog. She found him staring at the door leading down to the bakehouse, and every hair on his body was standing on end.

18

Molly squatted close to Angus. He stopped barking, though he continued to growl at the door.

"What do you hear?" she whispered. She put her ear to the door, but clearly whatever had upset the dog was beyond her human senses. Molly reached into her pocket, but her phone was missing. She tried to remember where she had set it down. Had she dropped it in the park? She remembered putting her hands in her pockets for warmth at one point.

Angus returned to his frenzied barking, now scratching at the door as well. Molly thought about the bakery office and the landline inside, but she couldn't bring herself to walk away from the door when Angus was so certain something lay on the other side. *What if an intruder hears Angus and decides to come upstairs to silence him?* She grabbed a long umbrella from the stand not far from the door, called herself an idiot, and opened the door. Angus was out of the apartment like a shot.

Molly gripped the umbrella and crept down the stairs, reminding herself that she needed to watch for flying objects. *Why am I going downstairs when I should be hiding in the office?* She could hear her brave little dog barking from somewhere in the bakehouse and suffered a sudden mental picture of the intruder kicking Angus.

She picked up her pace and soon reached the downstairs hallway, where Sean Mitchum stood not far from the back door trying to shake Angus off his ankle. The little dog had the man's pants leg tightly in his teeth.

"Don't you dare hurt my dog!" Molly yelled, rushing at Mitchum. "Angus! Come here."

Angus reluctantly let go of the man's leg and jumped clear of the kick that the intruder aimed in his direction. He backed toward Molly, but kept growling.

"Me hurt him?" Mitchum huffed. "This horrible mutt has bitten me twice now, and that doesn't even count the bite I got from that monster at the bookstore."

"*You* attacked Myron!" Molly yelped.

"If you mean the bald guy with the monster dog, no, I did not. They attacked me. I wasn't hurting anyone."

"You were breaking into the bookstore," Molly said. "Again. This time to leave that threatening note."

"I thought I ought to make sure you and your doe-eyed friend knew how much I wanted what belongs to me," the man growled as he took a tentative step toward Molly. "Now hand over that dog statue you bought at the bookstore. I know the goods must be inside."

"Not going to happen." Molly held up the umbrella like a baseball bat. It was a good umbrella, and she would give the man a serious smack if he came in range. "And the police are on their way." Molly passionately wished the lie was true. In her head, she made a promise to never be so reckless again.

Then to her absolute shock, the back door flew open and Fergus rushed in. "Get away from her!" he shouted.

"I'm not the one with a weapon here," the intruder protested, waving a hand at Molly.

"Only because Laura put away the kitchen knives," Molly snapped as Fergus slipped around Mitchum to get between him and Molly.

Mitchum eyed the back door. If he was planning to make a run for it, he gave up that idea when Officer Michael Drummond charged through the open doorway. "Hold it right there," the officer said. "You're under arrest, Mr. Mitchum."

With a groan, the intruder raised both his hands. "I only wanted what was rightfully mine," he said sulkily. "And all I've gotten is attacked by dogs. I'm the victim here."

"You?" Molly was astounded at the man's nerve. "You wanted your grandmother's jewelry so much you were willing to kill a man who only wanted a quiet retirement. That doesn't make you a victim."

"Kill?" the man yelped. "I didn't kill anyone. I didn't even hurt anyone—not on purpose anyway." Drummond was trying to get Mitchum's attention so he could read him his rights, but the man seemed completely focused on Molly.

"So if the knife you threw at me when you broke in here had hit me, that wouldn't have been on purpose?" Molly shivered, recalling the memory of the blade stuck into the wall so close to her head.

"Just try and prove that was me," Mitchum said with a sneer that Molly knew meant he had been the one to break in. "Anyway, you can't pin a murder on me."

"Why not? You definitely almost killed Myron Webster!" she insisted.

"The bald guy?" Mitchum shook his head. "That was self-defense. I didn't even mean to hit him. I threw a brick to keep the dog away. Have you seen that monster? It's not my fault the owner stepped right in the way. It wasn't meant for him."

"Actually, it *is* your fault." Officer Drummond finally got the man's attention by grabbing his arms and cuffing him.

Now restrained, Mitchum stopped arguing and glared at Molly sulkily as the officer informed him of his rights. "I didn't kill anyone," he grumbled when Drummond finished. "You'll see. I'm an innocent man."

"Hardly," Molly said. "The shock of having you break in killed Edgar Richardson. He was a nice man, and he deserved better."

As Officer Drummond was trying to guide the intruder toward the door, Mitchum planted his feet and shouted at Molly, "I had nothing to do with that old guy's death! He was dead when I got there. I worked around him, hunting for my grandmother's jewelry. She meant for me to have it. She did. They're family heirlooms."

That explained the angry message scrawled on the wall of the bookshop, Molly thought. Mitchum had been seeking what he considered his rightful inheritance.

The officer finally hauled Mitchum through the door, practically lifting the lighter man off his feet. Drummond called through the doorway, "I'll be right back after I secure the suspect in the car."

As soon as quiet settled on the bakehouse, Fergus put an arm around Molly's shoulders. "Are you all right?"

Molly suddenly remembered the kiss and gently eased away to shut the back door. "I don't want to end up chasing Angus around the neighborhood," she explained. Like all of her friends, Fergus sometimes put an arm around her, but now the gesture seemed too charged with meaning. "Why are you here?"

"I skipped out on the Valentine's event," Fergus admitted. "Neil had it well in hand, and I wanted to come and talk to you. I know things are still weird after that kiss. I don't want this awkwardness between us."

"That will take a little time," Molly said quietly. "But it'll be okay. I'm sure of it. We've been friends for so long. Why didn't you call to say you were coming over?"

"I tried," he said. "You didn't pick up."

"Oh. I couldn't find my phone."

He pointed through the doorway into the kitchen. "Is that it?"

Molly saw her phone laying on one of the worktables. She didn't remember taking it out of her pocket when she came in with Angus, but she'd been all over the bakehouse, so clearly she must have. Realizing she'd misplaced her phone without noticing hammered home just how tired she was. "I'm lucky you came by," she said. "I assume you called the police?"

Fergus nodded. "I was outside for a while, pacing. I was nervous about making things worse between us. That's when I saw Mitchum breaking in. I called the police, then I came in."

"I'm so glad you were here."

Anything else they could have said was interrupted by the return of Officer Drummond. "Molly, I'll need you to come down to the station and make a statement," he said.

"Do you think he's telling the truth about Edgar Richardson?" Molly asked. "Maybe Edgar had a heart attack before Sean even got there."

"I suppose it's possible," the officer said. "But you'd be amazed at how few murderers are eager to admit to the crime. I'm surprised he hasn't tried the accident excuse for Edgar Richardson. It wouldn't work though. We know his death wasn't an accident. The coroner found an injection site and the toxicology report came back. His heart attack was induced."

"Oh no." Molly raised a hand to her mouth. She realized a small part of her had held on to the hope that Edgar's death was an accident, something terrible yet unavoidable. But now she knew someone had killed him intentionally. Was that someone Sean Mitchum?

"I can see the wheels turning in that head of yours," Officer Drummond said severely. "You really do need to stay out of the investigation, Mrs. Ferris. I'm confident we have our culprit. You can go back to being a mild-mannered baker."

Molly resisted the urge to make a face at his slightly condescending tone, and Fergus spoke up before she could form a retort. "Thank you, Michael."

"You're welcome," Drummond answered. "Oh, and Officer Anderson said you have a journal that belonged to Edgar Richardson you were going to bring in."

"That's right," Molly said. "I'll bring it in the morning so you don't have to wait for me to go upstairs and find it."

The expression on the officer's face suggested he knew she was stalling for one more read of the journal, but he clearly didn't want to leave his suspect alone in the car any longer. "If you don't show at the station, I'll be by to pick it up."

With a tip of his head, the policeman left. Fergus followed him to the back door and examined the lock. "It doesn't seem to be broken. He must have picked it." He frowned at her. "Did you engage the dead bolt?"

"Maybe?" Molly's brain had been well and truly scrambled ever since the kiss. She needed to get her head on straight. She'd left her phone downstairs and failed to lock up properly even though she'd made a special point of it. She could have gotten hurt, or worse.

Fergus frowned. "It's not like you to be so absentminded."

"No it's not." Molly sighed. "I'll lock up tight as a drum and do nothing but read until bedtime."

"Are you sure you shouldn't call Carol or Laura?" he asked. "I'm sure they'd come over."

Molly sighed. "They would, and they'd fret and fuss over me. I don't need that. The bad guy is finally arrested." Her eyes widened as she had a thought. "I should call Chelsea and let her know. It'll help her feel better too."

"If you say so, but I'm going to check all your locks before I go. No arguments. Then I'll listen to be sure you lock the dead bolt this time. You need to take care of yourself, and Angus." At the sound of his name, the Scottie yipped in agreement.

Molly didn't bother arguing and followed Fergus around as he locked up. As soon as he'd left, she went upstairs to find the journal. She wasn't sure she was up for more journal reading after such a stress-filled day, but she could use the copier in the office to print the pages. That way she could hand in the journal and read the pages at her leisure.

As she began the tedious process, Molly put in a quick call to Chelsea Lowell. "I wanted to let you know the man who broke into the bookstore has been caught."

"Really?" Chelsea's voice was breathy with relief. "Are you sure?"

"I was here when the police led him away."

"Here?" Chelsea echoed. "Where?"

"Bread on Arrival. He broke in searching for something he believed your uncle had."

"Do you think it might be some evidence from one of Uncle Edgar's cases?" Chelsea asked.

"No, it wasn't related to your uncle's past as a policeman. The man simply wanted something he believed was in those cardboard boxes he destroyed." Molly considered telling Chelsea about the toxicology report on her uncle's death, but she decided that the young woman should hear it straight from the police, who could better answer any questions she had. Plus, she hated to do anything to destroy the relief in the young woman's voice.

"I'm glad the man is under arrest," Chelsea said fiercely. "I hope they throw the book at him. Thank you for telling me, Molly. I know I'll sleep better tonight."

"You and me both," Molly agreed before wrapping up the call.

The copying took longer than she expected, and she was more than ready for bed by the time she finished stacking all the printed pages. Not wanting to forget to take it to the station, she carried the journal out to leave it near her purse. That was when she heard Angus barking and growling from the kitchenette.

"What now?" she moaned. At least the kitchenette was a secure room, so surely Angus hadn't found an intruder. Unless it was a mouse. "Please, not mice."

Fortunately, Angus wasn't barking at anything living. He'd spotted the dog statue on the counter. With the stress of the break-in, she'd completely forgotten to retrieve the dog and jewelry for the police.

"I guess I'll have two things to take in tomorrow," she said aloud. Angus ignored her and continued to bark at the statue.

"It's a fake dog," Molly said. "Honestly, Angus, ignore it."

Clearly he planned on doing no such thing. Molly opened a cupboard and shoved the dog inside, leaving the packet of jewelry still on the counter to remind her to gather it in the morning.

With the dog out of sight, Angus gave the cupboard one more warning growl before he left the kitchenette in a huff. Molly walked to her bedroom with her phone in hand to plug it into her phone charger. With her scatterbrained behavior that evening, she didn't want to risk letting the phone go dead.

When the phone in her hand rang suddenly, Molly almost dropped it, stark proof that she was still extremely on edge. She looked at the phone and saw the number wasn't one she recognized. "Hello?"

"I know you have the ceramic dog," a woman's voice snarled. "You will hand it over or end up as dead as the bookseller. Got it?"

19

"Who is this?" Molly demanded. "I'm calling the police right now!"

"You'd better not," the woman said. "I know where you live, Molly Ferris. And that dog should never have been yours in the first place. It was stolen property, and you'll return it, or else that statue won't be the only lifeless doggy."

"How dare you threaten Angus," Molly snapped. She was absolutely going to call the police now. She'd made enough silly moves lately.

"Just bring that dog statue to the graveyard at St. Andrew's Church," the woman said. "Leave it at the feet of the stone angel with the sword in her hand. Do it now, and don't call the police. I'll know if you do, and I can promise you'll pay."

Molly had had enough of this, and she couldn't hide her annoyance. "I'll bring the statue, but then I'm done. If I even suspect anyone comes near the bakery or my dog, I won't be the one paying."

The woman hung up.

True to her own plan, Molly immediately called Greer's cell phone. "I'm sorry for not calling the department," Molly said when she'd filled Greer in. "But the caller seemed so sure that she would know. I'm worried she may have someone there spying and you won't be able to catch her."

"A woman?" Greer said thoughtfully. "I thought Michael had settled this when he picked up Mitchum. Who could this woman be?" Greer paused only a moment before she asked, "Could it have been Chelsea Lowell?"

"No, definitely not," Molly said firmly. "I would have recognized her voice. And the caller sounded older."

"Listen, Molly, I'm going to do the drop. We're about the same height, and if I wear your clothes and put on a hat, no one will be able to tell the difference in a dark cemetery. I assume you have the item the woman asked for?"

"I have more than that. The woman doesn't really want the dog statue. She wants the packet of jewelry that was inside it. I found it earlier this evening."

"Haven't you been busy? Okay, in case there *is* someone watching the police station, I'll meet you at the corner of Loch Ness Lane and Highland, and we'll make the swap. I don't want you anywhere near this person."

Molly could see the reason in Greer's plan, but she hated to miss out on seeing the woman who had called to threaten her. She was tired of feeling scared—for herself and Angus. But she agreed all the same.

Soon she was bundled up and driving the short distance from the bakery to the meeting spot with the ceramic dog and Edgar's journal on the passenger seat beside her. The packet of jewelry was nestled in the pocket of her coat.

As she neared the street corner, a woman in a long coat rushed to the passenger side of the car and hopped in, landing on the dog. The sudden movement made Molly gasp. *Had the stranger figured out their plan?*

"Ow, Molly!" protested the hitchhiker.

"Oh, it's you, Greer," Molly said as the officer retrieved the ceramic dog and book from beneath herself and set them on the dashboard. "I'm sorry for the rough landing, but in my defense, I didn't know you planned on jumping in."

"Of course it's me." Greer examined Molly with concern. "Molly, have you had enough sleep lately?"

"Clearly not." In the tight confines of the car, the women wrestled out of their coats and exchanged them.

"Okay, I'll take the dog, and you'd best give me the jewelry as well," Greer said as she pulled a hat down over her hair.

"It's in the pocket of my coat," Molly said.

Greer removed the napkin-wrapped bundle and peeked inside, raised her eyebrows briefly, then returned it to its hiding spot. She picked up the journal for a moment, then sighed. "You'd better keep this. I don't have a place for it, and I'm going to walk to the cemetery from here. I *will* be picking it up in the morning, though. Now go home and be safe."

Molly tossed the book into the back seat. "Please be careful."

Greer flashed her a grin, her teeth bright in the shadows. "Always." She hopped out of the car and strode down the street.

As Molly started her car, she watched the officer disappear around a corner. She knew Greer wanted her to head back to the bakehouse where she'd be safe, but Molly needed to see who had dared threaten her and Angus again. She quickly made a decision. She parked in the lot at the long-closed Loch and Key, choosing a spot out of the easy line of sight of the road. Then she wrapped Greer's long coat tightly around herself and headed for the churchyard at St. Andrew's.

When she reached Highland Street and passed the town hall, Molly marveled at the audacity of the woman who'd called. The church was within visual distance of the town hall, which included the police station. The caller lacked sense, but she certainly didn't lack nerve.

When Molly reached the church, she crept into the old graveyard slowly, keeping close to the bordering pine trees that offered a little cover. She'd been here before, but in the dark it was hard to remember exactly the direction of the angel statue with the sword. She expected to spot Greer moving between the graves, but the churchyard was perfectly still in the weak light from the moon.

"What do you think you're doing?" a voice growled.

Molly whirled to find herself facing a tall, sturdy woman she didn't recognize. "You called me?"

"I did," the woman said. "But this isn't the angel."

"I got lost," Molly stammered.

"And lost the dog as well?"

"I hid it close by," Molly said. "I can tell you where, but I wanted to avoid having you knock me over the head and leave my body while you ran off with the dog."

The woman smiled, and the shadows gave the expression a sinister twist. "And what's to keep me from doing it after you tell me where the dog is?"

Molly shrugged. "At least I'll see it coming. What do you want with the dog anyway?"

"Only what's coming to me," the woman growled. "For services rendered."

With that, Molly realized who was standing there. "Ida Paterson," she whispered.

The woman sneered. "You're not as stupid as Sean said you were. Though I suppose he's proved who the stupid one is here with all his dumb antics, breaking into places where he knew we wouldn't even find the dog just to be a menace. He's got some anger issues."

Mitchum wasn't the only one with ill intentions. "You were Emily Finch's nurse," Molly said. "With such a selfless calling, how could you get involved in something so self-serving?"

"Nursing wasn't my calling, it was a way to pay the bills—barely. And I did a good job. I deserved more for it. Sean agreed and promised me a healthy cut if I helped him find the jewels. Now I won't have to share them at all."

"How did you know the jewels were in the dog?" Molly asked.

Ida chuffed a laugh. "The old lady told me. She said all her worldly wealth was guarded by the family dog. She thought it was funny since she didn't have a real one. I thought she meant they were in one of the creepy dog statues the old bat had in her garden. I destroyed all of them before I realized it must have been in the ceramic dog from her bedroom. By then, the dog had been packed up by the estate sale people. The dog you bought, according to that credit card receipt we found at the shop. So where is it?"

"Right here!" Greer Anderson said from behind her. The nurse whirled, and Greer tossed Ida the dog before pulling her service weapon and training it on the woman. "And you're under arrest."

At that moment, Officer Drummond trooped out of the darkness to help. After reading the nurse her rights, he added, "You might think about this: it's going to be a competition to see which of you gives evidence against the other and gets the best deal. Personally, I'm betting on Mitchum. He's the weaselly type. It always goes easier on the one who talks first."

Molly stood perfectly still, hoping the officers wouldn't remember that they had a civilian audience and shoo her away.

"What's to say?" Ida demanded. "You heard everything I know."

"You can tell us which of you injected Edgar with the lethal dose of potassium chloride," Greer replied. "You're a nurse. You'd know that would bring on a heart attack."

"You're not pinning that on me!" Ida shrieked. "I wasn't even there when Sean broke into the bookstore."

"So you only gave him the syringe and told him how to use it?" Drummond asked.

"No, and that's all I'm saying." Storm clouds churned in Ida's eyes. "I want a lawyer."

"Then let's get you down to the station," Drummond said, hauling on the woman's arm. "You'll get one there."

Molly watched Michael lead the woman away. "Potassium chloride is what poisoned Edgar?"

"Yes, but don't spread it around. We try to keep *some* secrets," Greer told her as she shrugged out of Molly's coat and offered it back to her. "Not that it matters, since I'm sure we have the case locked up now. There's no more question of how Sean Mitchum would lay hands on the stuff or know it was deadly. His accomplice was a nurse."

Molly removed Greer's coat and swapped it for her own. "They both deny it."

"That's what criminals do."

Molly nodded reluctantly. Sure, she would have appreciated having everything tied up neatly with full confessions, but she needed to put the matter behind her. The police were confident and she trusted them. Didn't she?

20

By Sunday morning, Molly had mostly convinced herself that the death of Edgar Richardson and everything that had happened since was a settled matter. Still, she found herself distracted more than once during Reverend Findlay's sermon. As the service drew to a close, Molly whispered a quiet prayer of apology for her inattention before she stood to leave.

She had reached the aisle when the sound of someone saying her name finally cut through her distraction. She spun around to see Fergus's sparkling blue eyes and smiling face.

"I thought maybe you were ignoring me," he said.

"No, not at all. I'm a little preoccupied today. It's not you."

"I'm so glad. What's your plan for the day? Want to come home with me and be slobbered on by a giant dog while I fix you Sunday brunch?"

"You do make that sound appealing." Molly noticed that her conversation with Fergus was drawing attention. "We should chat outside."

"Sure." Fergus took her elbow in his hand as they moved up the aisle. "What has you so distracted?"

"Well . . . I got a phone call last night after you left," Molly answered, realizing Fergus was probably not going to be happy with this story. "Hold on until we are out of this crowd and I'll tell you."

"You certainly know how to build suspense." When they reached the foyer, Fergus pulled her to one side. "Let's chat here where it's still warm. What call?"

Molly explained about Ida Paterson and her effort to get the jewelry Mrs. Finch had stashed in the ceramic dog. Fergus grumbled a bit when she confessed to not following Greer's directions, but he held his peace throughout the retelling.

"I assume Greer and Michael told you what a bad idea it was to go into the cemetery," Fergus said finally.

"Actually they were a little busy arresting the woman." Molly held up her hand as Fergus drew in a breath, probably to launch into a scolding. "But I completely see the error of my ways."

"Which won't slow you down for a moment next time," Fergus said.

"Next time?" Molly grimaced. "I was promised that everything is settled and done. Despite what Ida or Sean argue, the police believe they poisoned Edgar. The case is closed."

"Mostly."

Molly jumped in surprise as Greer approached them.

"I need that journal, Molly," she said. "Is it still in your car?"

Molly nodded. *And the printed pages are in my coat pocket.* During a fit of guilt over printing a copy of evidence, Molly had decided to hand the pages over with the journal. She had folded the pages and put them in her coat, but the guilt had passed. She wanted to go through the pages one more time.

"I'll walk you out then." Greer turned her attention to Fergus. "I hope I'm not interrupting anything."

"A Sunday brunch invitation for Molly," Fergus said. "For which I still haven't gotten an answer."

"It sounds nice if there's some flexibility in the timing," Molly admitted. "I want to run by the hospital and check on Myron. It'll be a quick visit. I can call you when I'm done."

"No problem," Fergus replied. "Actually I'd love to hear that Myron will be released soon, before my new roommate eats me out of house and home."

"In that case, I'll head out with Greer," Molly said, noticing the police officer shifting impatiently. "And I'll call you."

As they walked, Molly asked Greer, "Have either Sean or Ida cracked yet and admitted poisoning Edgar?"

Greer shook her head. "No, they're both hiding behind lawyers and sulking. But it's a problem for the courts now. I feel good about the case."

They reached the car and Molly handed over the journal. She could almost feel the copied pages burning in her pocket, but she stuck with her decision and didn't mention them. "Sorry to take so long to get this to you. I don't think it'll be worth much as evidence."

"Then it shouldn't be a big problem that the chain of evidence is a mess." Greer took the journal. "Next time, remember evidence is for police."

"Of course," Molly said meekly.

Molly spent the drive to the hospital rationalizing the copied pages in her pocket. She doubted the police were going to give the journal much attention, and it never hurt to have an extra pair of eyes. After all, she wasn't keeping the police from examining the journal—not anymore anyway.

She arrived at the hospital fifteen minutes ahead of visiting time, and the older man at the visitor's desk refused to give her a badge until the scheduled time had officially begun. "Rules are rules," he said firmly before pointing at a small collection of chairs not far from the front door. "You can wait there. Fifteen minutes isn't long."

"Of course," Molly said. She found the chairs uncomfortable and the small waiting area drafty. She pulled her coat tighter around herself and dragged the journal pages from her pocket, hoping to distract herself from the chill as she waited.

Molly flipped through until she found the page for Edgar's first day at the farmhouse. She smiled sadly as she read what he'd written. It was clear the retired policeman was thrilled to be in Loch Mallaig, though he did find the town a little odd.

I know I'll get used to small town life where everyone expects you to know who they are, he wrote.

My neighbor is an excellent case in point. He was clearly offended that I didn't recognize him. "Don't you know who I am?" he asked, as if I were a long-time Loch Mallaig resident. I assume he must be some local celebrity, perhaps a retired mayor or some such. I find politicians often have delusions of grandeur.

Molly pondered the words on the page. She hadn't heard anything about Myron being well-known in the area. If anything, she suspected he was a bit of a loner. Whatever could he have meant? Molly decided to ask him about the reference.

She checked a large clock on the wall and saw that visiting hours had finally started. When she walked to the counter, the man behind it behaved as if he'd never seen her before, making Molly dislike him the tiniest bit more. He reluctantly handed over a badge, and Molly headed for Myron's room.

To her surprise, she found Myron dressed and seated in a chair beside his bed. He beamed brightly at Molly as she came in. "Is your friend here?" he asked. "I wanted to ask when I can come and pick up Bernie."

"Fergus isn't here, but I can call him if you want. I'm sure Bernie will be thrilled to see you. I have other good news too. The police caught the man who struck you and his female accomplice as well.

They're fairly certain those two broke into the bookstore and killed Edgar Richardson."

Myron's face darkened as she spoke, a direct contrast to what she'd expected.

"Is something wrong?" she asked. "I thought you'd be pleased to hear the police found the person who hit you."

"Of course," Myron said flatly. "It sounds like they did their job. That's all that's required of them, isn't it?"

Molly blinked, completely confused by Myron's attitude. If she'd been hospitalized after an attack, she'd be happy to find out her assailant was in jail. She wasn't sure what to say, but Myron must have sensed her discomfort as he changed the subject.

"I am extremely grateful for the kindness of your friend," he said. "I know Bernie isn't a dog someone takes home easily."

"Fergus has a big house," Molly said. "And a big heart." As she said the words, she knew they were true. Despite the awkwardness between them, she was incredibly grateful to call Fergus MacGregor her friend.

"No doubt," Myron said agreeably. "My Bernie has a big heart too."

"Angus and Bernie hit it off well. Must be their similar loving hearts." Then Molly abruptly changed the subject. "Do you mind if I ask you something?"

"Of course not. What can I do for you?"

"As it turns out, Edgar Richardson left a journal." Molly nearly stopped talking as Myron's face went blank again, his emotion unreadable. Since she could hardly leave the remark hanging, she pressed on. "He mentioned meeting you, and apparently he wondered if you were a retired mayor of Loch Mallaig. Have you ever held public office?"

Myron's face lightened, and he actually laughed. "Hardly. I'm not the political type, not that I don't admire Mayor Calhoun. He seems a good sort. I'm content to be a quietly retired pharmacist who stays busy reading, gardening, and walking Bernie."

"That sounds like a lovely life," Molly agreed, though she did wonder about Myron's annoyance with the bookstore. *How could anyone hate a bookstore when he listed reading among the three things he does with his time?* "Well, let me call Fergus for you and ask about Bernie." Molly pulled out her phone.

As soon as he answered, Molly put Fergus on speakerphone. "I'm at the hospital with Myron," Molly said. "He'd like to know when he can come by and pick up Bernie."

"And I want to say thank you for looking after my lad," Myron added.

"I'm happy to have had the company," Fergus replied. "He's a great dog. I'll be home all day, so you can come by whenever you're up to it."

"I'll come as soon as I get home to my car," Myron said. "I need to call a cab now, and who knows how long that will take. I also need to sign the discharge papers for the hospital, but they haven't brought them by yet. As soon as that's done, I'll be on my way home to get the car."

"You don't need to call a cab," Molly said. "I can drive you home."

Myron smiled. "That's kind of you."

"Once you drop Myron off, will I be seeing you, Molly?" Fergus asked.

"I'll run by the bakehouse and get Angus if you don't mind," Molly replied. "Then I'll head straight there."

"Angus is always welcome. I'll see you then."

A nurse walked in with a clipboard as Molly was ending the call. Myron eagerly signed the papers, then chafed at the idea of waiting for a wheelchair. "My legs work," he grumbled. "I would prefer to walk out."

"Sorry," the nurse said. "It's hospital policy. But someone will be by shortly. Consider it a little ride on us."

Again Myron grumbled, sounding so surly that Molly fleetingly regretted offering him a ride home. The man certainly had a quickly shifting temperament. He stayed sulky while they waited for the attendant with the wheelchair. Molly tried to strike up a conversation to take his mind off the wait, even mentioning Bernie, but nothing seemed to brighten the man's face.

"Are you in any pain?" Molly asked finally, wondering if a headache was the cause of Myron's gruff disposition.

"I'm fine," he snapped. Then he blew out a long, impatient breath. "I'm sorry. I shouldn't take my impatience out on you. I hate hospitals. I always associate them with death."

"I think that's what they're trying to help patients avoid," Molly said.

"Yeah, I suppose." He peered at her sharply. "So do you still have that shopkeeper's journal?"

Molly shook her head. "I handed it over to the police. I doubt it'll affect their case against Sean Mitchum or Ida Paterson. It's mostly a record of his days since coming to Loch Mallaig and a little bit of his work as a police officer."

"And you read it?" Myron asked.

"Mostly."

From his expression, Molly expected another question, but the hospital attendant arrived with the wheelchair. The attendant pushing the chair was about the same age as the grumpy guy at the front desk, but he couldn't have been more different in attitude. He joked and chattered during the whole walk outside. Myron never replied to his comments, so Molly made it a point to respond pleasantly.

By the time they reached the car, Molly was looking forward to the end of her time with Myron. She'd endured enough of his grouchy company for one day. The attendant watched as Myron settled himself in the passenger seat, then he wished them a good day and strolled off with the wheelchair. Molly noticed Myron didn't respond to the man's cheery goodbye either.

She slipped into the driver's seat and smiled at Myron. "I'll have you home in a jiffy." *And it can't be soon enough.*

"We're alone now," Myron snapped. "You don't have to pretend anymore."

For a moment, Molly wondered if Myron had realized how weary she was of his attitude. "It's all right," she said soothingly. "I understand the grouchiness. You've been through something of an ordeal."

He huffed. "Don't condescend to me. I know you've figured it out. But who have you told?"

Molly stared at him in confusion. What was he talking about? He seemed to be confessing something, but she had no idea what. Could Myron have been involved with Sean Mitchum's plan? How many coconspirators did the man have? "I have no idea what you're talking about."

Suddenly Myron shifted position and shoved something into Molly's ribs. She tried to see what was in his hand, but the folds of her coat hid it from her view. Still, it wasn't comfortable.

"Mr. Webster! What are you doing?"

"You're going to drive me out to your boyfriend's house," he snarled. "And we'll talk to him about what you both know. And don't try anything cute if you want to survive this trip."

"Please," Molly sputtered, her mind racing as she tried to figure out what secret Myron thought she'd learned about him. Although her thoughts were a jumbled mess, one stark realization floated to the surface.

Myron had murdered Edgar Richardson.

21

Myron rammed the object into her side. It hurt sharply, suggesting a bruise at the very least. Molly yelped, and Myron snarled, "Drive. Now!"

With her hands clutching the steering wheel, Molly's mind raced. She was driving a killer to Fergus's house. The guilt from that thought almost drove out the ache in her side, which was made worse each time Myron grew frustrated and jabbed the weapon against her. Though the situation was overwhelming, certain details slowly began to edge through Molly's panic.

What was the weapon in her ribs? It couldn't be a gun. He'd never have gotten one into the hospital. She thought for a moment that it was a knife, but the end was too blunt to tear her coat or draw blood. She was going to have a bruise, but no wound. That meant whatever he was poking into her side wasn't all that sharp.

As that thought became clearer, she realized that it was unlikely he would have had access to anything sharp in his hospital room. In fact, there was every chance she was being menaced by a butter knife from his dinner tray.

Did that mean she should stop the car right there and call his bluff? That thought was far from appealing. He was still bigger and stronger than her. But he certainly wasn't bigger and stronger than her and Fergus combined. She loosened the grip on the wheel slightly. She could get through this.

"So exactly why did you kill Edgar?" she asked boldly. "Surely not because he opened a bookstore."

Myron snorted. "Hardly. He killed my brother, so I killed him."

Molly gasped in shock and risked a brief glance away from the road to gawk at Myron. "You're telling me that Edgar Richardson was a murderer?"

"As good as," Myron growled. "My brother was an idiot, for sure, and a thief. But when Edgar arrested him, he clearly didn't pay proper attention to George's health. If he had, he would have gotten George a doctor. My brother died from a massive heart attack in some squalid jail cell. So you see, what I did was justice. An eye for an eye."

"And a heart attack for a heart attack." Molly remembered the discussion she'd overheard at the hospital. "In the hospital, you said you take something to manage the side effects of your blood pressure medication. I'm assuming that's potassium chloride. How did you know it would induce a heart attack?"

"I was a pharmacist," Myron snapped. "Pay attention." He followed that admonition with a fresh jab in Molly's side that made her yelp again. There was definitely going to be a bruise when this was over. She only hoped that was the worse that would happen.

"Why did you think he'd recognize you?" Molly asked.

"I was at my brother's inquest. I heard Richardson testify, but apparently he paid no attention to George's grieving family. No attention at all."

"I'm sorry," Molly said, hoping to build a little rapport and possibly weaken the jabs in her side.

If Myron heard her, he didn't react. Clearly his attention was on the past. "I kept waiting for him to recognize me after he moved in. Bernie and I passed by the bookstore over and over. I even sent him a note telling him I'd never forget what he did. But nothing. Then the man began viewing me with amusement. Can you imagine? He was entertained by my hatred."

"I'm sure that's not—" Molly broke off with a cry as he poked her again.

"I'd finally had enough, so I took the syringe with me on my walk with Bernie. I expected the bookstore to be closed, but there you were, you and that other woman. I thought you two would never leave, but you finally did. I walked right in with Bernie. I asked that old fool if he recognized me then. He treated me like some kind of kook, a joke. So I told him. I reminded him about George, but he refused to take responsibility. He was *doing his job*, he said. As if that absolved him of guilt."

"Edgar wasn't a small man," Molly said. "How did you manage to inject him?"

"He lost interest in me," Myron growled. "He said some rubbish about my picking out a book or letting him close up, then kept on sorting through those infernal boxes. He didn't even look at me. So I slammed the syringe into his neck. He saw me then." The smile on Myron's face from the memory gave Molly a cold chill.

Finally Molly steered onto Perthshire Lane. Fergus's house was less than a quarter mile away. "We're almost there," she said. Guilt washed over her again. She didn't think Myron could do Fergus much harm with whatever he'd been jabbing into her side, but she was definitely bringing trouble right to her friend's doorstep.

Fergus threw open his door and led Bernie out as soon as Molly drove onto his property. At the sight of the car, Bernie began straining at the leash. Fergus waved at Molly before using both hands and all his weight to keep the dog next to him. Molly felt like crying from the guilt.

"Don't say anything to tip him off," Myron warned. "Get out."

Myron threw open his door and stepped out. Molly opened her door slowly and clambered out, her eyes on Fergus. Her expression must have been telling, because she saw confusion and concern pass over his face.

Myron had circled the car at a trot, and grabbed Molly's arm. *What am I going to do?*

She never had a chance to figure that out. Fergus had realized that something was very, very wrong, so he simply let go of the huge dog's leash. Clearly Bernie was the one element Myron hadn't considered. His dog crossed the space between Fergus and Molly at a speed that was nearly terrifying. He slammed into Myron with the full force of his considerable weight and knocked the man flat. Then he stood over him with paws on his chest, licking his face with slobbery enthusiasm while Myron sputtered and struggled.

Molly spotted Myron's weapon laying in the dirt near his hand and scooped it up. As she'd thought, it was one of the dull knives from a hospital food tray.

Fergus rushed to Molly's side. "What is going on?"

"Myron killed Edgar," Molly said. "We should call the police."

They did, then merely let Bernie sit on Myron until they came. Myron did his best to push the dog off, but Bernie had missed him and refused to be dislodged. When the police arrived, Molly and Fergus worked together to lure the big dog away so the police could cuff the slobber-covered murderer.

Fergus's expression darkened when Molly described the kidnapping to Greer, and Molly thought fleetingly that it was lucky for Myron that he wasn't on the ground anymore. He might have gotten a good kick. But maybe not. Fergus wasn't like Myron, she reminded herself. He would never give in to a thirst for vengeance.

Greer's expression grew sheepish when Molly ended her story. "I'm sorry," the officer said. "I thought we had our killers with Sean and Ida. I never would have suspected this guy."

"I probably wouldn't have either," Molly admitted. "But his own imagination led him to believe I already knew."

After stowing Myron in the car, Officer Drummond had joined the others while Molly was talking. "I always say criminals aren't too bright. If they were, they wouldn't be criminals."

"I certainly hope this is over now," Fergus said. "Molly has been through enough."

"And I have the bruise to prove it," Molly said, rubbing her side and wincing. She regretted that instantly, as everyone chorused insistence that she be checked out by a doctor. She agreed reluctantly, wishing she could just put the entire experience behind her.

By the time she got home from the hospital, she was starving, a feeling made worse by the delicious aromas coming from the food Fergus had picked up on the way.

"At least I can let Angus out into the yard again," Molly said. "Which is good, because if I had to walk him before eating, I would collapse from hunger."

"I could walk him," Fergus said.

"Haven't you had enough canine care for the week?" Molly asked. "I imagine walking Bernie must have been a challenge."

Fergus groaned. "And now I don't know what to do with that dog. He's a two-time hero, so I can't surrender him to a shelter. He deserves better. But my house already needs a steam cleaning, and I'm not home enough for a dog as attached as Bernie."

As Molly turned the key in the lock, a thought popped into her head. "I may have the perfect solution."

Nearly two weeks later, Molly stood in front of Books & Bargains with Angus and Bernie at her side while Chelsea Lowell loaded her suitcase into the passenger side of Edgar's SUV. The younger woman patted the roof of the car. "When I came out here, I never would have thought I'd be exchanging my compact car for this tank. I'm lucky it was part of my inheritance."

Molly handed the big dog's leash over to Chelsea. Angus whined softly when Bernie lumbered to Chelsea's side, putting distance between them. Molly felt a little sad for Angus. He would miss his new friend. She nodded toward Bernie. "I'm afraid a Newfoundland isn't a compact car dog."

Chelsea stroked the big dog's head. "No, he certainly isn't. He's my big ol' hero dog, aren't you, Bernie?"

The dog's tail swept the air like a sail and the gaze he pointed toward Chelsea was adoring.

"I didn't feel safe after my uncle was murdered," Chelsea said. "But Bernie changed that. Between the bad guys going to jail and Bernie being my watchdog, I slept like a baby here every night. And he was good company while I went through Uncle Edgar's belongings. The task felt so daunting when I first moved here from the guesthouse to tackle it. But the last two weeks went by in a blink. And now it's time for us to get back to real life."

"I know he'll appreciate having a good home with you in Illinois," Molly said. "All Bernie needs is someone to love him."

"He'll certainly have that with me—love and a big couch." Chelsea smiled, but it faded to seriousness. "I've thought a lot about Myron. At first, I was so angry, but he must have been really messed up over the death of his brother. I can sort of understand that—not the desire to kill someone, but the grief. I think with time, I'll be able to forgive him and feel it."

"And that's why you and Bernie will be a great team," Molly said. "You both have big hearts."

Chelsea grinned. "Bernie has big everything." She gazed

affectionately at the farmhouse for a moment. "I'm going to miss Loch Mallaig, but it doesn't make sense to keep this place. My life is in Normal."

Angus was still whining softly, clearly sensing something was happening that he wasn't going to like. Molly bent and scooped him up, giving him a hug.

"You're always welcome to visit," Molly said. "I know a lot of people who would be glad to see you if you do."

"I'll keep that in mind." The young woman's smile grew a little sad. She reached out and patted Angus's head. "Bernie and I should be going."

Molly held up a finger. "I think there's one more thing we should discuss."

"What's that?"

"I might technically be the owner of Emily Finch's jewelry since it was inside the dog I bought from your uncle. But I believe you're the rightful owner since Ed bought the statue legitimately from Emily Finch's estate sale. I'll make sure it gets to you once it's released from evidence."

Chelsea put up a hand. "I can't keep it. That doesn't feel right."

Molly bit her lip. "It wouldn't feel right for me to have it either."

After a few moments of silence, Chelsea's face lit up. "Let's put it into the hands of a good jewelry auction and sell it, then donate the money to a dog rescue in honor of Mrs. Finch. I've spoken to a few people around here who knew her, and it sounds like she truly did love dogs."

"I'm sorry I never met her," Molly said. "From everything I've heard, I would have liked Emily Finch a lot."

"Anyone who loves dogs is all right with me." Chelsea ruffled Bernie's ears. "Isn't that right, sweetie?"

Bernie whuffed deep in his chest, and Chelsea giggled in delight. Watching Chelsea and Bernie together, Molly was struck by how different they were, but how perfectly they fit together. *Like Angus and me*, she thought, giving her little dog another hug. Angus lapped at her chin and Molly knew her own fond smile mirrored Chelsea's.

"I'd say we both have a lot to be grateful for," Molly said, mentally making her own list that began with Angus and included all the wonderful people in her life as well. "After the last few days, I'm really counting my blessings."

"I am too, thanks to you," Chelsea said. "I lost sight of them for a little while, but I don't think I'll forget how very blessed I am anytime soon. Bernie will make sure of that."

Bernie whuffed again as if he was in complete agreement. Chelsea loaded the big dog into the SUV, then hopped in herself. She waved at Molly through the glass before starting the car and pulling away.

Angus whined again and Molly gave him another hug. "How about we take a special trip to the dog park and visit with some of your local furry friends?" she asked him.

At the words "dog park," Angus's little tail began to wag and he wriggled with anticipation, making Molly laugh. Angus was never down for long.

"That's right, Angus," Molly said as they walked back to her car. "You and me, we're never down for long."

Angus yipped in happy agreement, ready to face whatever came next in his day. And Molly realized she felt exactly the same way.

Up to this point, we've been doing all the writing. Now it's *your* turn!

Tell us what you think about this book, the characters, the bad guy, or anything else you'd like to share with us about this series. We can't wait to hear from *you*!

Log on to give us your feedback at:
https://www.surveymonkey.com/r/ScottishBakehouse

Annie's® FICTION